I0573294

The Nymph's Labyrinth

Danica Winters

CRIMSON ROMANCE

F+W Media, Inc.

Published by
Crimson Romance
an imprint of F+W Media, Inc.
10151 Carver Road, Suite 200
Blue Ash, Ohio 45242

www.crimsonromance.com

Copyright © 2012 by Danica Winters

ISBN 10: 1-4405-6223-7
ISBN 13: 978-1-4405-6223-5
eISBN 10: 1-4405-6224-5
eISBN 13: 978-1-4405-6224-2

This is a work of fiction. Names, characters, corporations, institutions, organizations, events, or locales in this novel are either the product of the author's imagination or, if real, used fictitiously. The resemblance of any character to actual persons (living or dead) is entirely coincidental.

Dedication

*To Bridget and Gavin—
May you always follow your hearts.*

Acknowledgments

I want to thank my critique partners and dearest friends Casey Dawes, Rionna Morgan, Clare Woods, and Pam Morris. Your constant support and kind words are invaluable.

I also want to extend thanks to Amanda Luedeke who always has my best interests in mind. I can't wait to see what the future will bring.

Also, thank you to Jennifer Lawler for extending a welcoming hand.

Lastly, I want to thank my family (Eliot, this goes for you too) and friends—your love and humor keeps me on my toes.

PROLOGUE

The Palace of Knossos, Crete
1613 BCE

Zeus stepped to the side of the bed and lifted the sheet to gaze at Epione's sleeping form. The goddess's hair splayed around her head in a black halo, and her hands rested over her bare breasts. The warm ocean breeze filtered through the curtains behind him as he stared down at her tanned chest while it rose and fell with the innocence of sleep.

The air must have startled her and she stirred. The nymph's hands shifted from her breasts as she moved to stretch, and the action made the God's manhood quiver to life. He dropped the sheets back down and as the air wafted against her skin, she opened her eyes. "Hmmm. Zeus?" She yawned. "Have you come to me in need of healing?"

Epione sat up, pushed her legs out from beneath the bedding and stood up. Zeus' gaze fell to her round breasts and trailed down to the black wavy hair between her thighs. "I come for deeper needs. Needs only a woman…no, only a nymph can fill."

She stumbled toward her robe that lay draped over the wooden chair at the end of the bed, but he put out his arm, stopping her. "You won't be in need of a covering."

She glared at him as she backed away from his touch, and bumped against the wooden bed behind her. "What of your wife? She'll be angry if you stray from your marriage bed, will she not?" Epione pulled her hair over her shoulders and covered her chest.

"Are you not the goddess of all nymphs? The Queen of the seductresses? Is it not your job to soothe a man? I am here to be a victim of your seduction, to have the needs of my manhood and my aching desires sated by your touch, not to worry about the fickle emotions of my wife."

"A man who treats his wife with such indifference will find no place in my bed. I believe in true love, not infidelity."

"She cares not where I plant my seed—only that I return to her." Zeus reached out to touch her. "Come here and show me how you seduce, then I will leave and you can find another man who you can *love*."

He laughed at the thought of such a romantic idea. Who wouldn't want a nice tussle without the attachments of love? And the Queen of seduction? She would most certainly be in need of good lovemaking. He would love to teach her the ways of a real God.

Epione stared up at him with her bright green eyes. She was even more beautiful than the other gods of Olympus had foretold.

"I know who you are, and of your erotic escapades. I wish only to be made wet by those who love me eternally, not those who wish to ravish me for sake of their fantasies." Epione turned to the bed, grabbed a sheet and pulled it around her. "I seduce and soothe whom I choose."

Zeus ran his fingers along the edge of the white sheet, so close to her breasts. So close to possessing what his loins called for. Her denial only made him want it more. "I am a God. I have sired gods and goddesses, and ruled humankind. Having me as a lover is an honor. There's no reason you should not choose me." He leaned closer to her, and could smell the salty scent of her skin. "My body is ravaged with pain of want and only you can dampen my fire."

He followed her gaze toward the corner of the room, where a crystal staff shimmered in the sun, but he cared nothing of her trinkets, only the purpose that pulsed from between his thighs.

She sat down on the edge of the bed, careful to keep her body covered. "You'll need to find another to wet your fire."

Anger flashed within him. *Who does she think she is?*

He reached toward her, but she pushed his hand away. "I am a god. The *God* of gods. I ravish whomever I desire. My touch is an honor to those with whom I share my bed."

With a calm fury, she flung aside the sheets, pushed up from the bed and sidestepped around him. He turned as he watched her grab the crystal staff.

She glared at him with a fury reminiscent of the fires of Hades. "Let me be the first to be dishonored."

Zeus stepped back and lightening sparked from his fingers. His body responded with a hardness that came to the men of war. "I will not beg. You'll give me what I want, or I will take it."

Epione thrust the staff in the direction of his manhood. "Come near me and I'll burn it off."

He covered his groin and sneered. "Your denial will bring only acrimonious dishonor."

"So be it." She jabbed the staff at him again.

He glared at the idealistic goddess. "Because of you, your kind will be cursed. Never again will you or your kind partake in your senseless desire for *true love*. If a nymph attempts to love a human, that man will be fated to die a tragic death!"

"No." The crystal staff lowered as she shirked from his words.

He raised his arms to the sky and bellowed. The ground quaked beneath him. "This island and everything you hold dear I condemn to the fires of Thera. All because you dared to turn a god away!"

"You wouldn't!" she cried. "What of the humans?"

"The Minoans worship the bull, not the God of gods. They deserve no mercy."

The walls cracked and fissured around them as the earth shook. Thunder filled the air and from the window, a cloud of gray ash poured from the direction of the volcano to the North.

"Foolish Epione, you and all that your humans hold dear will this day be destroyed."

Chapter One

Present Day

Shoveling dirt in a dark, forbidding hole was the last place Ariadne Papadakis wanted to be. She used the trowel in her hand as a weapon to scrape the clay away. A drop of sweat trickled down the ancient black tattooed snake on her arm, past her elbow, over the serpent's weaving body, and stopped at the base of her wrist as if it was afraid to enter her palm where the head of the snake was poised for attack.

The city of Gournai sat at the base of a Cretan hill, a blister of light in the callous night. Ariadne could remember when the town had been nothing but a few villas and a market, perfectly rural—a great location for a secret. Now it bustled with modern life and somewhere within the public maze, sat an archeologist who wanted to expose the Labyrinth she and her sisterhood of nymphs had kept hidden for so long.

How had Beau Morris found their secret…a secret that had been hidden for thousands of years? She couldn't know for sure, but now she had been ordered to deal with the consequences of his action.

Earlier that day, while Ariadne had been working at the museum in Heraklion, a braying couple from Alabama had been among the handful of visitors. They had laughed at the bare breasts of the statue of Epione, the snake goddess. They had snickered and made jokes of the serpents that graced her arms and her ample breasts. They never paused to consider what the woman had once meant to so many and still meant to Ariadne's sisters and all nymphs. They had just laughed and gawked at the oddity before them. Stupid Americans.

Did no one revere what is sacred anymore? Had culture changed that much?

Ariadne pushed the thoughts from her mind. There were some things about the modern world that she just didn't understand, and Dr. Morris' ardent desire to destroy the nymph culture by exposing the secrets of the Labyrinth was at the top of her list.

Couldn't he just leave some things alone?

If he found the Labyrinth, the artifacts would sit in the museum, and like the statue of Epione, be pointed at and mocked—or they would be misused. The sacred Labyrinth needed to stay exactly as it was, hidden from science, from prying eyes, mocking laughs, and greedy hands.

She jabbed the trowel into the hard earth.

The trowel-marked square walls around her seemed to move in a little closer as Ariadne worked. She swallowed back her fear as she looked up at the night sky. When she was done, she could get out of this place and never come back.

Her gaze fell to the exposed light gray column at her right. For a moment she stared at the moonlit carved stone, it reminded her of the thousands of years that had passed since she had been born. Each year brought a new challenge, a new set of problems. She ran her finger against the arid dirt and brought her fingers to her nose to smell the burnt sage, the citric aroma of oranges, and a hint of olive.

To have an archaeologist sticking his nose where it didn't belong was an invasion tantamount to war. Subterfuge was the game and nymphs had thousands of years of practice.

The ocean breeze picked up and with the scent of salty air, came the dank, putrid scent of forbidden secrets. A hooded crow called out, announcing the arrival of night and sordid undertakings, and pushed Ariadne back to work. She needed to complete her task and get out of the depths. She needed to get back to Heraklion, back to normalcy and out from under her sisters' command.

The tip of the trowel struck gray volcanic ash and Ariadne stopped. The top of the Minoan-era dirt sat exposed and vulnerable. Ariadne grabbed the box beside her and pulled off the cardboard lid. After she slid on a pair of latex gloves, she lifted the tiny skull and placed it in the hole.

Lifting the rest of the bones one by one, she laid them beneath the skull. Ariadne thought of the child to which these bones had once belonged. She and the child must have been alive at the same time. Had she seen the little one playing in the fields or at the market? Maybe the child would like the mischievous game she was playing, but only if she was successful.

It was of no use to wonder about the past. Now these were just bones, and the child's spirit was alive and well in the heavens.

Ariadne moved on to the ribs, lying one bone above the next. In no time, she was done. After all, the skeleton couldn't be too perfect. This was supposed to be a body that had been resting beneath the earth for thousands of years, not a freshly sown grave.

Satisfied, Ariadne pulled the sweaty blue latex from her fingers and stuffed the gloves into her back pocket. Grabbing her trowel, she carefully pushed the soil over the body and packed it down.

Perfect.

The roar of a car stopped her in her tracks. Looking up, Ariadne watched as headlights bounced off the edges of the pit above her. Her heart pounded.

Damn it…someone is coming.

Grabbing the box and trowel, she stood up. Standing on her tiptoes, she grabbed the edge of the pit and peered out into the night. A thickset man had his back turned to her as he opened the rear door of his car. For a second, she could only stare at the man, his snug American jeans, and his gray T-shirt that stretched over the well-defined muscles of his arms. He brushed his shaggy hair behind his ear.

Breaking her gaze, Ariadne stuffed the handle of the trowel in her back pocket and pushed the emptied box under her arm. The dirt from the edge crumbled beneath her fingers as she pulled away. Stumbling backward, she shoved her body into the tight space between a column and the earthen wall.

Hopefully he wouldn't come into the pit where she was hiding. A confrontation wasn't ideal. No, it was supposed to be in and out, as Kat had instructed.

Ariadne tried to slow her heart as she stood still, a human bridge between the memories of the past and the terror of the future. So much was at stake—her life, her culture, her species.

The car door slammed shut and crisp footsteps approached the pit. Ariadne pushed her body back as far as it would go against the crumbling wall. The tight space made her heart race faster, and a bead of sweat slid down her forehead—she was a trapped animal.

So…tight. She must stay calm.

He moved closer, and her breath quickened. She needed to get out. Though he couldn't kill her if he found her, trying to explain her presence would be next to impossible.

Shifting was an option, to strike at him with her serpent fangs—a couple of well-placed bites and he would no longer be a problem. But to kill…it was so permanent.

I shouldn't have come here.

She sat the box down in front of her feet and closed her eyes. Shifting was the only option.

Shuffling her feet, they scraped against the dry soil. Her eyes sprang open. The sounds of the man moving toward the pit stopped.

"Who's there?" the man said, his smooth voice breaking the tense silence.

Ariadne didn't answer. Holding her breath, she peered out from behind the column. A pattering rain of dirt announced the man's entry into the pit. His thick, brown hair shimmered in the moonlight and silhouetted his V-shaped torso.

The beam of his flashlight bounced around the cave, and she pulled back, deeper into the small space.

The light moved away from her and she peered around the darkened corner. The man's back was to her, as he faced out into the night. His feet were in front of the disturbed patch of soil, but he didn't seem to notice. *Thank the gods.*

Pulling the trowel from her pocket, Ariadne sat it on the ground. Closing her eyes, her arms pulled into her sides and her legs blended together. Her teeth grew longer and sharpened in her mouth. There was a quiet thump as her clothes fell to the ground. The man turned toward the sound as her body dropped to the ground.

The light flashed above her, but he must not have seen her and he turned back.

Her smooth body snaked around the cardboard box and past the edge of the column as he pulled a bottle from his pocket and took a long drag.

The ocean wasn't far. Beau's body would be easy to hide.

Chapter Two

Beau Morris threw his feet up on the cheap particleboard desk of the rented room. A roach scuttled across the floor. Without thinking, he pulled his boot from his foot, and pitched it at the bug, missing the roach by at least a foot. He'd never been much of a baseball player; books and dirt had always been more of his thing.

God, he hated this place. He should have been with his field crew. Instead, he was pent up in this hellhole with nothing but a roach for company.

His mind wandered to the young students. Each morning at least one or two of them staggered into the site still stinking of booze from the all-night parties. Maybe there was something to staying in the roach-infested room. At least he had his own place, a place where he could come, relax, and think about the site instead of babysitting all day and night.

Opening up his laptop, he scanned through his emails. Bills, bills, and more bills. Clicking through the mess, he paid the ones he could and avoided the ones that could wait. At the bottom of the list was an email from Lynda. It wasn't time to pay yet, but without a doubt she was stepping in line for her money.

Without opening the email, Beau clicked to his account and sent the normal amount. That should shut her up for a while. Avoiding her at all costs was the simplest solution. He always seemed to trip into disasters when it came to her. The only thing good about Lynda was Kaden.

Watching his son ride his first bike had been a great moment.

What has it been? Ten years? Kaden must not be much of a kid anymore.

Even if Beau didn't get to see him much, it was still a comfort to think that he had a boy running around. Especially a boy who loved to cause his mother a little bit of hell—Lynda deserved every second of his orneriness.

When Beau had emailed Lynda about the possibility of bringing Kaden to Crete, Lynda had seemed to consider it, but she had decided against it. Kaden didn't know him, and a summer in another country would have been a disaster. On the other hand, it would've been fun showing Kaden the site and taking him to Heraklion, where there was a fantastic museum.

Kaden might've loved Crete, he could have taken part in the dig, helped his old man. Not that he was old; nah, thirty-four was only slightly worn. There was plenty of life left in him.

Closing his email, Beau opened up his site files. There were so many loose ends, but with a little luck, they would find what he was looking for, he was sure of it. Then the National Science Foundation would get off his back. All he needed was something to prove his theory. Something tangible and the NSF would be eating out of his hands.

Next to his computer, the newspaper sat partially unfolded. There was a picture of the Cretan riots, where the unemployed picketed around a building. He scanned to the next page. He couldn't help but snicker at the headline. It said it all, "Archeologist Searches for Answers." They didn't know how right they were. Questions were easy to come by, but answers…they never seemed to come.

Beau took a sip of the beer sitting next to the paper and sat it on top of the headline. A drip fell from the bottle and splashed against the paper, blurring the ink.

The NSF was never going to give him the grant for next year if he didn't get his crap together.

A knock broke the silence.

Who would be at his room at this hour? Maybe one of his crew members? God only knew what trouble they had caused.

Last week, the police had been called for a broken window. The offending student had to pay for the window to be replaced, but at least Beau had managed to get the charges dropped.

"Who's there?" Beau grumbled as he stood up and grabbed his boot.

No answer.

Goddamn college students.

The person knocked again.

"Hold your horses. I'm coming. I'm coming." Beau's ankle cracked as he slipped his boot back on.

Wiping his face, he shook out his hands and then reached for the doorknob.

The person banged again. *Geezus, what could be so goddamn important?*

Opening the door, his jaw dropped.

A black-haired teenager looked up at Beau and pulled his orange backpack a little higher on his shoulder.

What the hell? Kaden?

"Hey kid…buddy," Beau stuttered, trying to cover his shock. "What're you doing here?"

Leaning out the door, Beau looked out into the hallway. Except for the two of them, the hall was empty.

Beau grabbed Kaden's shoulders and led him inside. "Where's your Mom?"

"She's probably at the airport by now," Kaden said, with an unemotional shrug. "She brought me here and then when we were about to come inside, she disappeared. She was in a big hurry to get on her honeymoon."

"Honeymoon?"

"Yeah, Beau. I guess you didn't get the email. She got married a couple days ago."

Since when did *his son* call him "Beau?" He looked over at the boy he had only known from school pictures and five-minute phone calls for the last ten years. The pictures of a smiling, polo shirt-wearing young kid didn't match the pierced, black-haired, hoodie-wearing teen that stood in front of him. How had Lynda allowed this to happen?

"Did she say when she would be gracing us with her presence?"

"Hey, old man, I just followed her here. We didn't talk a whole lot."

Old man? Geezus, this situation was worse than he had thought.

The door clicked shut behind them, and Beau's gaze wandered to the beer on the desk. Trying to be subtle, he walked over and grabbed the bottle and stuffed it into the back of his pants. He wasn't a great dad, but even he knew beer and kids didn't mix.

"You have another one, *Beau*?"

Beau grumbled, unsure of how to respond.

Kaden had to be trying to irritate him. *No wonder Lynda dropped his ass off. When is she coming back?*

Then Beau remembered the email. Maybe it hadn't been for child support, but why hadn't Lynda called? A man needed a little warning that a juvenile delinquent was going to appear on his doorstep.

Kaden walked to the bed, dropped his backpack to the floor and flopped down. "Is this it? This is where I'm gonna be living? I thought you were some famous scientist or something. This place is a shit-hole."

Living? Huh.

"Don't you think you need to watch your mouth?"

Kaden's eyebrows flipped up in mock surprise. "You think I give a shit about what you think, old man? Did you forget that I haven't seen you for ten years? You're the last person who is going to tell me how I can and can't talk."

Great…so this is how it's going to be.

His son didn't have a clue about the history between him and Lynda, but it hadn't been Beau's fault that he couldn't see Kaden.

But Kaden wouldn't understand. He was too angry, too young.

"Look kid, we can get along or we can call your mother and get her to come back here. I think it's great you're gonna…live here… but there's got to be some ground rules."

"Go ahead and call her." Kaden pulled his MP3 player out of his bag and shoved in his ear buds. "She won't answer. I already tried."

Lynda would never change. It was and had always been the selfish path of least resistance with that woman. And again, Kaden was the one paying the price.

*

Governor Kakos' office door was closed, but the sound of giggles penetrated into the waiting room where Ariadne stood. Without knocking, she pushed open the door to his office.

The blonde secretary leaned over the governor's desk, her breasts inches away from Stavros' tan face, while her fishtail skirt inched closer and closer to showing the world her well-known secret.

Ariadne stepped into the lust-scented room and clicked the door shut. The woman stood up and straightened her skirt, causing her breasts to press hard against the buttons of her jacket.

Ariadne could pretend to be upset or jealous, but it was too much work. Stavros was Stavros; if he wanted to screw the whole island, he would.

"Hello, Ariadne," the woman said, patting her hair.

"Bunny," Ariadne responded with a slightly annoyed nod. "Stavros, you and I need to talk."

Stavros' gaze flickered to Bunny, and a tiny spark of guilt played on his face. If Ariadne hadn't known him for years, she wouldn't have noticed the subtle way his eyebrows trembled, or the way he licked his lips when he had done something wrong. The man hated uncomfortable situations, but like a true politician, he tried to brush off his guilt by acting apathetic.

Stavros stood up from his desk and buttoned his gray suit jacket over his flat stomach. He pulled his sleeves down and walked to the door with a smug grin. Opening the door, he motioned for Bunny to leave.

Walking out, Bunny looked over her shoulder and directed a sultry smile back at him.

Ariadne rolled her eyes. *Really? It isn't like Bunny needs to broadcast their affair.*

Stavros turned from the door and smiled. "Aria, I'm glad you stopped by."

Of course he wouldn't say anything about what just happened. "Hi, Stavros."

He looked Ariadne up and down with his brilliant green eyes. "You look exquisite today."

Without waiting for her to respond, he walked across the room to her. He smiled and brushed his thumb over her cheek, then leaned in for a kiss. She let her lips touch his, but she felt nothing, just a stagnant familiarity.

Forcing a smile, Ariadne walked away and sat down in the leather guest chair. "Well, Stav, I need a little favor."

Stavros walked to the small mirrored tray that sat in the corner of the room. He lifted up a crystal decanter and poured himself a drink. Taking a sip, he turned back and walked to her side. He put his hand on her shoulder and gulped the clear liquor. "Like?"

Reaching up, she put her hands on his. "We have a bit of a problem. An American archeologist is too close to the Labyrinth. We need to shut him down before he finds anything *inconvenient*."

"Hmmpf." Stavros pulled his hand from her shoulder.

He walked over to the other side of the desk and sat down. His glass clinked as he plopped it on the wood of his desk.

He wasn't going to go along with this, but she needed to try.

"First the protests and now this. How much is this problem *we* are having going to cost me?"

"It's not a money thing. I just need you to put a stop on the project."

Stavros' manicured brows rose. "Which one?"

"There's an archeologist, Dr. Beau Morris, working in Gournai. I went there to stop him last night, but I think this is beyond my… ability."

Killing was best left to the wicked.

"Oh, come now," Stavros said, his eyes straying down to Ariadne's breasts. "You have *ample* abilities."

Of course Stavros would think it had to do with her ability to seduce. He would think Ariadne would turn to sex to handle every problem. "So you are saying you want me to *use my abilities*?"

"Hmm…" He smiled. "It is nice. This *thing* we have. Hate to change up a good thing."

He took a long drink. Leaning in, she let her cleavage spill over to sweeten the deal. She took the glass from his fingers, took a drink, and slid it back toward him.

"Look Stav, we both know what he will find if he keeps digging. You need to stop the work."

He set the glass down on a little round coaster. "Aria, have you talked to Kat about this?"

"Kat thinks it's best. She was the one who sent me here. We don't want anyone snooping around the group right now." Her heart leapt into her throat as she thought about Kat. If Kat found out she had resorted to using Stavros to handle the problem, there would be hell to pay. "We can't risk exposing ourselves or the magic of the Labyrinth. What happens if someone figures out you have an island filled with nymphs?"

"One thing is for sure, it would increase tourism. The money would come piling in." Stavros' eyes gleamed with greed.

"Yes, and you would risk yourself and everyone *different* just to make money. You know how humans react to things they don't understand. Besides, there are better ways to draw people to the island, less dangerous ways."

"Like what? The economy is struggling. We need something big, shake things up a bit. Get our economy running strong again. Think about it. We could draw millions with just the headline, 'Mythological Seductresses Exposed,' or even better, 'Labyrinth Found Filled with Priceless Treasure.'" Stavros laughed at his sick joke.

"You know we can't do that, Stavros. We can't let Dr. Morris find the Labyrinth."

"Just because he finds the Labyrinth doesn't mean he will expose nymphs. Just—"

"No," Ariadne said, cutting him off. "If Epione's crystal staff is found, that's worse than nymphs being exposed. At least we would stand a chance. We could disappear. But if you give the power of the staff to humans, you would start something none of us could hide from."

Stavros shook his head. "You're right. I'm just throwing ideas around here."

"Tell me you will shut down the site."

He took a long swig from his glass. "I can't shut it down without a reason, Aria."

She smiled wickedly. "The reason will be exposed soon enough. I've already made sure."

Chapter Three

A black-haired teen coughed into his elbow as he sprawled across one of the museum's observation benches. The sound echoed through the empty exhibition space.

Ariadne pulled down her sleeves as she walked up to the young man. With an acknowledging nod, she sat down. The teen pulled his hood off and looked at her with curious brown eyes. "Hey."

She smiled. "Hello. What're you doing?"

He pulled his arms more tightly across his chest. "Nothing," the teen said in an American accent.

Pain radiated from him. His loneliness and anger were palpable. "How do you like the museum?" Ariadne asked, trying to force him into a conversation. "Did you see the double-headed axe when you came in?"

"Fine."

In front of them sat a rock crystal rhyton. The pitcher was one of the most beautiful things in the museum, yet the boy didn't seem to notice. "Did you see the double-headed axe when you came in?"

The boy shrugged.

"What's your name?" Ariadne tried again.

"Kaden."

"Well, Kaden, my name is Ariadne Papadakis. I'm the curator for this museum. And I never want to see someone not enjoying themselves in such a magical place."

"I'm okay."

She smiled at his obvious lie. "How long have you been in Crete?"

"A couple days."

"Is this your first trip?"

Kaden nodded.

She looked around. The museum was quiet today, as it had been for the entire summer. "You're lucky you get this place all to yourself today."

He looked around with a bored expression. "Yep."

She loved the museum, but she felt for the lone teenager who was stuck in a place he didn't want to be. "You wanna see something cool?"

The boy's eyebrows rose. "Like?"

"This place is filled with secrets, some for visitors and some just for staff. If you would be interested I could show you one of the secret rooms." Ariadne tried to bait his curiosity.

The teen looked around the room. "Sure. Let me just tell my dad, okay?"

Kaden stood up and as he did, a brunette man with a V-shaped torso walked into the room from the hallway. Ariadne's jaw dropped.

What is Beau Morris doing in the museum?

Beau looked her up and down with his alluring milk chocolate-colored eyes. A smile crept over his face. "Hello, Miss…" he said, gazing down at her chest. He pointed at her nametag. "Uh… Ariadne?"

She nodded, trying to hide her shock at seeing the archeologist again. His face was clean-shaven and his hair less disheveled than a few nights before. He had been handsome before, but now he was almost irresistible. No wonder she hadn't been able to kill him.

Beau walked closer to them and stopped next to Kaden. "Thanks for watching my kid." Beau reached up and put his arm over the boy's shoulders.

Kaden looked uncomfortable as he wiggled out from beneath the man's touch. "She was going to show me the most secret room in the museum."

Oh, not the most secret room. There is no way they could see the real treasure that sat beneath them.

Ariadne's cheeks flushed. Thankfully, they didn't seem to notice.

"Do you mind if I tag along?" Beau's eyes lit up.

From the way his voice vibrated with excitement it surprised her that he hadn't drooled at the prospect.

Ariadne looked at Kaden and then back at Beau. There was a striking resemblance between the two men. Except for the dyed black hair, Kaden was just a smaller, less eager version of his father.

The best thing she could've done was to say no, but seeing the way Beau looked so hopeful, she didn't have the heart to refuse him. Besides, there would be nothing beyond a quick trip to the storeroom.

Ariadne tried to smile. It was nice to have someone that truly appreciated history. So often the museum was filled with vacationers who came simply to point and laugh at the bare-breasted sculptures and the murals of the bull leapers, but why did the person who finally cared have to be the archeologist she had sworn to stop?

"Let's go." Ariadne pointed to the door to their right.

Beau ran his fingers over his sexy, disheveled brown hair and his hand came to rest on his tanned neck. "You sure? I mean I don't want to get you in trouble or anything."

She looked at him with a sideways glance. Kat had made him sound like he was a vicious predator, but the man that stood before her seemed far from the type. Instead, he seemed humble and almost a bit beaten down.

"You're fine. I run the museum." She walked to the side door and led them to the back store room.

"It must be nice not having to answer to anyone," Beau said in a tired voice.

Ariadne smirked. *He doesn't know anything about me.*

The temperature-controlled room was muted by the roar of the industrial fan. In the center of the room sat a large lab table and on top, the ceramic statue of her goddess, Epione, stood bare-chested, with a sacral knot at the center of her chest. She wore a floor-length skirt covered with a short apron and snakes wrapped around her elegant limbs as they extended toward the heavens.

"This is the Minoan snake goddess. Science doesn't know much about her, but I have to admit that she is my favorite piece. There are so many stories that can be assumed by her appearance." Ariadne looked over at Kaden, who stared at the figure. "Kaden, what do you think?"

Kaden stood silently for a moment and then looked up at her. "This's your favorite?"

Ariadne nodded.

"Why?" he asked, confusion in his voice. "I mean, why would you pick this old dirty woman? Here you got gold and silver…you know, priceless shit."

"Kaden, watch your language," Beau growled.

Kaden rolled his eyes and continued. "Besides from being old, she's kinda…well, ya know, boring. Why'd you pick her?"

Ariadne glanced over at Beau, who was staring slack-jawed at his son. "Well, Kaden," she started, "sometimes the things we know the least about are the things that most impact our lives."

Kaden shrugged. "I don't get it. I mean I guess she's great and all, but still."

"I think she's exquisite." Beau moved his hand toward the goddess and stopped short of touching her. His eyes were bright with wonder and reverence.

Something shifted inside of Ariadne as she stared at the handsome man, but she tried to force the feelings down.

Beau walked around the table as he studied the statue. "Do you mind if I ask to see what else you have from the Minoan era? I'm an archeologist. I think this type of thing is fascinating."

"An archeologist, huh? Where are you working?" Ariadne turned away in an attempt to hide her face.

Walking over to the wall, she pulled a bin from the shelf. He would like it, but in it he would find nothing she would worry about him seeing.

"Gournai." Beau grabbed the container from her and placed it on the lab table across from the snake goddess.

"Are you working near the palace of Knossos?" She tried to sound curious, though she knew the answer.

"No, a bit outside of the palatial zone. I've researched the area and, well, I found some interesting peculiarities." He chewed at the corner of his lip like a guilty child, trying to hide a secret.

"So how is the dig going, Beau?"

"Good. Today my assistant is having my students catalog last week's finds. Normally I head it, but I'm taking a few days off so I can show Kaden around the island a bit."

"That's really sweet." Ariadne looked over to Kaden, who was picking at his nails.

"Have you found anything of significant interest?" Her mind wandered to the tiny bones she had held in her hands a few nights before.

"We've found quite a bit. We located a previously unknown villa, but inside we've found only ceramics and a few pieces of bronze."

It was more than a villa. Was he being vague, or did he really think that it was just a simple home that he had stumbled across?

Beau looked away from her, picked up a vase from the container and rotated it in his fingers. On its surface was a painting of a bull and woman. He stared at the image and then looked up at her. "This woman looks like you."

Ariadne reached over toward the object and touching his hand, pulled the artifact into her view. She couldn't focus on the image, only on the warmth of his flesh beneath hers. The simple touch made her stomach clench. She dropped her hand. "Oh."

Why did I touch him?

Looking up, he was staring at her, his eyes wide.

Ariadne looked away. "So, what is, uh, the goal for your project?"

Beau flushed for a moment and sat the vase back in the container. "I think there's more to the Minoans than what we've found. Everyone talks about the Palace of Knossos, but the Minoans left behind legends that there are other places yet to be found. And I think all legends have some basis in fact."

Ariadne smiled. "Which legend, exactly?"

"One that involves your namesake," he said, looking pleased with himself.

"The Minotaur and the Labyrinth?"

His face twitched at her question. Even if she hadn't already known, his tell was obvious.

"You know that's only a myth, right? You can't believe everything you hear."

A half-grin flickered across Beau's tanned face, making him look incredibly sexy.

"That's a nice vase." He motioned to the container. "We're finding similar works at the Minoan level, but nothing that well-preserved."

Does he really think he is hiding something?

Ariadne reached over the edge of the container and centered the vase in its cushioning. Her sleeve moved up her arm.

"Hey." Kaden peeked over the edge of the container. "Sweet tattoo. When did you get it?"

She pulled her sleeve down over her wrist. "Thanks. I've had it a long time."

Kaden looked over at his father. "I think you should let me get a tattoo." Kaden smiled for the first time since she had met him.

"Is it a snake?" Beau asked, as he ignored his son's plea.

"Uh, yeah." She tugged her sleeve into her hand and covered the head of the snake in her palm.

Kaden eyed her with admiration. "You must really like the snake goddess."

She leaned in close to the teen and whispered so that only he could hear. "You have no idea."

Beau picked up another small vase and compared it to the first.

"Now, Beau." Ariadne stepped toward him. "About the Labyrinth. What pointed you in the direction of Gournai?"

The door behind them flew open. Ariadne turned around. Kat was standing in the doorway. Her mouth was open and her hand rested on her hip. "Ariadne…" she growled. Her gray eyes flickered with anger.

Ariadne looked at Beau and Kaden. "Sorry, gentlemen, but I think the behind the scenes tour is over."

"Thanks for sharing this with us, Ariadne." Beau sat the artifact down into the box. "If you want, you're welcome to come visit my site sometime. You might find something there that'll spark your interest."

"Yeah. You gotta come see it," Kaden added. "It's awesome."

A sardonic grin flickered on Kat's face. "Oh, don't worry, boys. Ariadne has a way of getting around. I'm sure you'll get a turn."

Chapter Four

Beau rubbed his hands together and looked at the place where Ariadne's fingers had touched his. It felt strange to be haunted by a memory that probably meant nothing to her. It was only an accidental touch. He closed his eyes and thought about her fingers, long and dainty, her skin soft. It would feel so good to have her run them down his skin, around his waist. He stopped himself. He was at work. This wasn't the time to daydream about some teenage crush.

The trowel whispered to him from his bucket of supplies.

"Hey, professor," his student, Vickie, called from the far side of the site.

With a quick wave, Beau turned his back on the over-eager young woman. His assistant could get the students running this morning. He needed to get his mind back on task and avoid all women for as long as possible.

He pulled out the trowel and sharpened the blade with a thick steel file. It was nice to finally be on site and back to work. It had been a solid week of tourist traps and dinners spent in silence, as Kaden looked anywhere but at him.

He needed this; to get his hands back into the dirt, to follow his dream, and make things happen. This had to be the place to find the Labyrinth, but if Beau didn't get back to work and find something he would never know…and he'd never have a job again. It was already a tough sell to convince the University of Texas that he was a worthwhile professor. Anthropology wasn't a field of study that many students were going into since the economy had tanked.

Not that he could blame the students for following more stable goals. All they had to do was look at Beau to know what a pipedream archeology was—only a few scientists could have ever been considered newsworthy. Most archeologists were just like him, scrimping by, begging for funds, or else working for states on building projects making sure everything was found in an area slated to be destroyed. At least he was on the conservation end of the spectrum.

There were a few professors back at the university who were doing well, but only thanks to their political ties and play-it-safe attitudes. Right now, they were probably sitting around, guzzling their chardonnays and laughing at what a fool he was for chasing the Labyrinth. No one, not a single professor, had taken him seriously when he had told them he hypothesized that the Labyrinth was real. Most thought it was nothing but a fantasy, like the Ark of the Covenant or Atlantis.

They didn't understand all the hours of research Beau had poured into the subject. He had gone over everything, old texts, excavations, and he had even managed to get his hands on a top-secret geophysical survey. Everything pointed to here, to this little point right outside of Gournai.

When he told his colleagues he was going after a grant from the NSF to find the Labyrinth, Professor Ryan laughed in his face, splattering him with the coffee the fat man had been holding in his mouth. The memory of Ryan made his gut clench. He had to prove them wrong and save his face and his job. The Labyrinth was here. He just knew it. He could feel it in his soul.

Beau looked out at the site. There were eight open sites, or digs. The students were climbing in and out of their squares, carrying dirt-filled buckets to the screens and filtering out the artifacts. Everything looked routine, even relaxed, but the students didn't know how close they all were to being shut down and having to go back to Texas with their dirt and sweat-covered hats in their hands. He would probably have to beg the dean to keep his job, and forget tenure.

He rubbed his hands against his face, trying to push the worries from his mind. He needed to dig; and his dig, dig three, waited for him.

Kaden was perched on the edge of the stone wall that ran adjacent to the site. "Kaden, do you wanna help me?" He pointed to his 12x8 square with the column by the back wall.

The boy said nothing. Beau stepped closer to the rock wall where his son was sitting, covered by the hood of his black sweatshirt. Beau looked over the side and followed Kaden's gaze. A group of teenage girls glanced up the hill and turned back to each other as they noticed him looking.

A young blonde girl wearing a white T-shirt looked up at Kaden and gave him a quick half-wave.

It looks like I'll be on my own today.

Beau smiled. "Why don't you go talk to her, Kae?"

Kaden pushed his arm over his mouth and coughed as he turned his back on the girls. "I don't think I should be taking dating advice from you; you didn't even make a move on the lady from the museum."

Should he have made a move on the curator? The kid must have seen signs he hadn't. The woman had treated him with a cold indifference, not a warm "come and get me" vibe. "Fine, kid. But I would think you would take this chance to get a break from your old man for a bit. You have been stuck with me for almost a week. This has to be different from staying with your mother."

Kaden turned back around to face the girls. "You're right," he said, standing up. "You're a lot easier."

A snort escaped Beau. *Easier? Really?*

He thought back to Lynda. Before they had divorced, she was always making promises to the kid when she felt guilty about some shortcoming. When she forgot him at daycare, she had promised him a new baseball mitt; when she missed his school's holiday performance, she had promised him a pricey video game that he had wanted. But she never followed through. Beau would try to cover for her and get the things she had promised for Kae, but it always seemed like Kaden knew that she had failed him. He couldn't fail his son in the same ways his ex-wife had.

Kaden pushed his hood down from his head and jumped from the short ledge, landing with a thump. He started down the hill.

"When are you going to be back?" Beau called after him.

Without looking back, Kaden shrugged.

"Well, we call it quits at five o'clock. Be back before we set to leave."

Kaden wandered down the hill toward the girls. When he reached them, Kaden stuffed his hands in his pockets and stared at the ground. The blonde girl twisted her hair in her fingers while she smiled sheepishly at his son.

A few hours later, Beau's back was sore from bending over and his knuckles were open and bleeding, but the pain felt good. He stood up to stretch just as a black town car roared up and parked next to the crew's rented vans.

A tall, athletic man in a gray suit stepped out. His black patent leather shoes glimmered in the sun. Slamming the door shut, the man looked in the side mirror, adjusted his suit jacket and tie, and patted his hair. When he looked up, he nodded at Beau. "Hello, Dr. Morris."

Beau squinted and moved closer to the businessman. "I'm sorry, do I know you?"

The man smiled. "I'm Governor Stavros Kakos. I've been hearing about your site and thought I'd come take a look for myself."

A blonde woman stepped out from the passenger side of the car. Her skirt was a red so bright it almost hurt Beau's eyes.

Governor Kakos pointed at the woman. "This is my personal assistant, Ms. Dover. You can call her 'Bunny.'"

Beau nodded a curt welcome. "Is there something wrong, governor?"

"No, no, no." The man smiled.

The woman walked up to them and touched the governor's arm. Governor Kakos glowered at her for a split-second, and then moved away from her hand. He looked up and smirked at Beau. Something about the way he looked at Beau, with a mixture of superiority and derision, made Beau's stomach sour.

"Actually, I've come here to speak to you about an issue we've been having. There've been some complaints about some of your students being a little disorderly in Gournai. Especially a Ms. Woods. There's been talk about her and some unseemly behavior." The governor's distasteful gaze never wavered.

Beau's blood pressure rose. His students were young and they liked to drink, but he hadn't heard of any "unseemly" behavior aside from the window, but that had been an accident.

But what if the NSF hears I'm having problems with my field crew?

"I'm sorry, governor. I'll have a talk with them. You won't have any more problems. I guarantee it." He looked over to the redheaded Vickie Woods, who was perched on the edge of her dig. She glanced back at them, as if she could hear what they were talking about.

"Glad to hear…" The man stepped around him and the woman trailed behind they walked to the edge of his dig. "On another subject, I was hoping to find out when you would be done with your little excavation."

The man annoyed him more by the second. If the man were anyone other than the governor of the region, he would have been back in his car along with his plaything.

"I'll be done when I find what I'm looking for," Beau answered, his voice sparked with unintentional malice.

The man's habitual smile flickered. "And what is it that you are looking for exactly?"

The governor must've known. He had signed the paperwork

months ago that allowed the dig. If he wanted answers, he could get his girl to find them out for him.

Then again, this was the man with the power to shut him down.

"We are hoping to find the Labyrinth, or a tangible indicator that it exists."

Bunny looked up at the man with a curious look on her face. Like a true politician, the man smiled placidly as he digested the information. "Crete is in need of tourism and tourism dollars—the protests are getting worse. If you find what you're searching for, you can greatly impact this island."

Of course the man would care about the money, not the cultural or historical impact of his team's work.

Beau mimicked the man's fake smile. "I hope so."

"As such, I'll let this dig continue." The man paused. "But if there are any more problems or complaints, I will be forced to reconsider my decision."

One more thing going wrong, how convenient…

The man began to stride away, but after a few steps, he stopped and turned back. "If you find anything of importance, I want you to contact me immediately." The man stuck out his hand and flipped a card on the ground at Beau's feet.

"Sure thing." Beau looked down at the card. Turning his back on the man, he walked to the main tent that stood at the far end of the site and held all of their catalogued finds. He didn't look back until he heard the car roar to life and drive off.

Just what I need—another person to answer to.

After checking on the students, he walked to dig three. When Beau jumped down, he caught sight of something blue from the far corner of the dig, behind the column. He walked over. Heaped in the corner was a pile of women's clothing with a blue latex glove poking out of the back pocket of the jeans.

He stooped down and picked up the clothes and stuffed them under his arm. The students bustled around him as he made his way to the dumpster. No one seemed to notice as he lifted the clothes and dropped them inside.

Maybe this was evidence of some of the "unseemly behavior" the governor had mentioned. But having a conversation with his students about who left the site naked didn't sound like Beau's idea of fun. Nor was talking to Ms. Woods about the governor's accusations, but he would have to. Hopefully it wasn't her who had left the clothes.

He searched for anything else out of order, or some evidence of looting, but everything was in order. Something didn't feel right, but he pushed the feelings aside. There was work to be done.

Sweat dripped down Beau's face as the afternoon wore on. He scraped away the soil and dumped it into the five-gallon bucket, making notes as he worked deeper. When the bucket was finally filled, he lugged it to the sifting screens. Vickie was bent over the mesh square beneath the wooden A-frame supports. Her red hair was pulled into a ponytail that stuck out the back of a University of Texas baseball hat. A dribble of sweat beaded on the back of her tan neck.

The day was getting hot, and having to talk to the woman the governor had labeled as having "unseemly behavior" only made the heat more sweltering. Confrontation twice in one day was wearing, but hopefully the governor had misunderstood—Vickie didn't seem like the type who would act out.

He sat the bucket down next to the screen with a thud, and Vickie looked up. "Hi, professor."

"Hey." He stepped to the opposite side of the screen and pushed his fingers through the clumps of dirt that sat on the metal mesh.

Damn, I hate this type of thing.

After a moment, he looked up at her. Her fingers fumbled through the dirt.

He couldn't bring himself to ask about the governor's accusations. "Have you found anything?"

God, sometimes I'm so weak.

Vickie looked up and smiled, her white teeth sparkled in the sun. "I found a coin, and a few bones, but the best thing was this rock." She grabbed a stone from the side of the square and held it up for him to see.

The gray stone was the shape of a heart.

He picked it up from her hand. The stone was smooth and polished—too perfect for a natural stone.

"This is a fantastic artifact. Nice find."

She laughed. "Thanks."

"Why are you laughing?"

She looked at him with her enormous brown eyes. "Because… you are holding my heart in your hands."

Oh, shit…

Beau laughed nervously and sat the rock down. Her eyes never left him and the action only made him more uncomfortable.

He turned away from her gaze. "I'll come back when you're done."

His heart beat fast and hard. Did Vickie just hit on him? Or was it a joke? He couldn't have a relationship with a student. It was unethical in every conceivable fashion, but her advance did something to him he hadn't felt since the day at the museum.

Walking to his dig, he stepped down into the pit. Standing there, he closed his eyes, and tried to remember Ariadne's face. He could see her golden eyes, her glittering smile, and the way her hair had fallen like silk over her shoulders. He needed to see her again.

No… He only had a month before the funding ran out. They were down to the last layer, his last shot to prove himself and his theory. He had to focus on work. He needed to find something—and it couldn't be a woman.

Picking up his trowel, he forced himself back to work. It would have been better if he was sketching or photographing the stratigraphic levels, but he needed to feel his muscles pull taut beneath his skin…anything to erase the thoughts of Ariadne from his mind.

Scraping, his trowel made an odd grating sound and he stopped. He pulled the brush from his pocket.

"Hey, Beau…" Kaden's voice broke through the muggy air.

Beau stopped. Standing up, he wiped his brow. On the edge of the pit stood Kaden and the girl he had seen eyeing his son. "Hey."

His son looked over at the pretty girl and dropped his gaze to the ground. Beau held back his smile. "Who's this?"

The girl extended her hand. "Hi, I'm Trina. Nice to meet you, Professor Morris." Beau took her hand and shook it, her grip was firm and she looked him square in the eye. "I hope you don't mind, Kaden said he would show me around your site." She leaned around and looked past him, in the direction of the center of the dig.

Kaden pulled at the back of his neck and fiddled with his hair. *Ah, young love.*

He envied their naïve desire to fall into a situation that would undoubtedly turn into a disaster.

"Yeah sure, go ahead," Beau answered, as he stared at the layer of soil where he had been digging.

Squatting down, Beau picked up the plastic brush. Feathering the bristles against the ground, the ash pushed back and revealed a face. As he removed more and more soil, he could see the tan of the woman's face and the dark paint around her golden eyes. Her lips were a subtle shade of red and her dark brown hair was swept up into the classical bun. Underneath her face, was a line of text. He recognized it as Linear A, but that was as much as he knew.

Sweeping away the dirt beneath the text, his hands began to tremble. Pressed into the tablet was a clear circle, inside of which were smaller and smaller circles all connected by lines. He traced the lines with his finger, some of the lines ended abruptly, while others arced and switched, then came to an end. Dropping the brush, he put his hands to his head.

He couldn't believe it. *Is it real?*

He ran his fingers against the stone and felt the coarse dirt beneath his touch. It was real. It was a sign. This small clay tablet was evidence…evidence of the Labyrinth. But he needed more.

Chapter Five

The dig needed to end. Beau Morris was charming and thoughtful, he listened and cared, and Ariadne couldn't be around him again. Everyone on the island had seen the morning's headlines that praised the work of the archeologist and his field crew. Stavros had even made a statement about how he intended to use the dig to create jobs, making it clear he had gone against her wishes to shut the project down.

This time she intended on making him listen to reason. He wouldn't dare expose non-humans—not if she had a say about it.

She walked into Stavros' office. Bunny's desk was empty and a giggle escaped from his inner office.

Not again…

Ariadne tiptoed to the office door. Touching the handle, she pressed it down, and slowly cracked open the door.

At the side of his desk was Stavros. His shirt was unbuttoned and his pants rested just above his knees. Bunny's bare legs were wrapped around his waist, and his hands hidden from sight.

Ariadne nudged the door open an inch more and could see him cupping Bunny's tanned breasts as she splayed across the top of his desk.

Ariadne pulled the door closed and turned to walk away.

Stavros has never portrayed himself as a saint. This day has been coming for a long time. He is a bull, for gods' sake. His animalistic urges drive him… But why today? Why when I need him, did things have to hit an all-time low?

What am I going to do now?

Going back to the site was too dangerous. What if Dr. Morris suspected her of something, or what if she inadvertently let something slip? The sisterhood wouldn't forgive her if she gave away their secret. And what would happen if he touched her again?

A chiding giggle echoed out into the main office. Anger twisted through her. Stavros wasn't going to get away with treating her like this anymore.

She turned back around and charged the door. Slamming it open, the handle smashed against the wall.

Stavros, mid-thrust, looked up. "Ariadne…" He thrust deeper. "Hello, lover."

She balled her fists. A thousand things ran through her mind. Should she yell and scream? Call him a liar and a manipulator? Should she slap him, or go after Bunny?

Stavros smiled. "Do you want to join us?"

Bunny looked up at her with a sickening smile.

What the hell did he think? Does he really expect me to run over to the desk and get to work?

"You have to be kidding." Ariadne strode to the center of the room.

Stavros pulled up his pants, but left the zipper open. "What? We've been together for years and the entire time you have been blind to my occasional indiscretions just like I've been blind to all of your little *seductions*. Why do you want to make a scene about this?"

Bunny sat up and pulled away from Stavros. Covering her breasts, she jumped behind the desk, away from Ariadne.

Ariadne smirked. That was the smartest thing she had ever seen that girl do. She turned back to Stavros. "I haven't seduced anyone in a long time. Don't you try to make this my fault."

Stavros leaned over, put his hands on the corner of the desk, and looked up at her. "You have the same needs as I do… Needs that we can't always fill for each other."

"I can't believe you."

He shoved off the desk with an angry force. "What? I wasn't made to be with one woman until the end of time. You know this."

She did know he was like a typical bull, strong, thickheaded, and driven by the dangling appendages between his legs.

Stavros walked over to the decanter that sat on the mirrored tray in the corner of the room. "Besides, you know you can never leave me. You and I both know that you will never have love."

Bunny's hands shook as she tried to button her tight white shirt.

He dropped a piece of ice into his glass and sloshed the ouzo over the little chunk. "Don't act like such a saint. Let's forget about this whole thing and have a little fun."

Ariadne looked back at Stavros. "There are no saints in this room. But I'm not interested in your impromptu orgy."

"Not that many years ago, you would have jumped at a chance like this. What's going on with you?" He tugged up the zipper on his pants.

"Nothing is 'going on' with me. I'm sick of you and your lack of respect."

Bunny adjusted her skirt as she stepped beside Stavros.

He lifted the crystal glass and took a long gulp. "Aria, I thought we had an understanding."

"What? That you could screw whoever, whenever—without a second thought for me and what I may think?" Her neck tensed and she could feel the start of a headache.

"That's not what I said…" He offered his glass to Bunny, who took it with a shaking hand. The secretary took a tiny sip, and then handed the oversized glass back to him. "You are being such a…woman. I thought you were better than this."

"I *am* better than this." Ariadne walked to the door and opened it. She glanced back over her shoulder at the sight of the two fornicators.

"Shut down the site, Stavros."

He pushed a pen straight on his desk. "I'll do what needs to be done."

*

Stavros and Bunny wouldn't care. They would never see or understand why Ariadne was hurt and angry. They were two people that were cut from the same cloth, they both wanted instant gratification, regardless of the consequence. Ariadne was the fool. At least she felt like one.

Stavros had let her down on so many levels. And now Ariadne was going to have to take care of the Morris situation herself as well. She should've never thought to rely on Stavros, he would use whomever and whatever he needed to get ahead—even her.

Thumping her elbows down on the café's table, she pushed her face into her hands and massaged her temples in an attempt to lessen the throb of her headache.

She was so angry, but mostly, she was angry with herself. She should have known after the way she had seen Bunny the first day at the office…she should have been prepared to one day walk in and find them doing what they had been doing.

Why me? Why have I never been able to find a man that cared for anyone besides himself?

"Ariadne?" A shrill voice invaded her senses.

She looked up, and standing in front of her, was the worst possible person she could have run into. "Kat," Ariadne said in a flat voice.

She looked past the woman wearing a wrinkle-free snowy white skirt and a yellow top and scanned the empty courtyard surrounding the outdoor café. At least Kat was alone, instead of with her little menagerie of followers.

"You seem absolutely *pitiful.*" Kat's lips were pursed as if she was trying to keep back a smile.

"Thank you. It's nice to see you, too."

Kat reached down and flashed her black snake tattoo as she pulled out one of the extra chairs. She slipped into the seat. "Is this all about that archeologist? How's it going, keeping an eye on things?"

"What? Yes, no…"

"I thought we talked about this. You need to get the site shut down, so whatever you need to do with Stavros, make it happen."

"Actually—"

"I don't want to hear excuses. I have my hands full, I expect you to be able to handle one little archeologist. Though I have to say, you seemed too cozy with him when I saw you two in the museum."

"Like I said before, that was nothing. I was throwing him off the trail. I didn't want him to get suspicious."

"You didn't want him to get suspicious of you—a woman he had never seen—by taking him into the back room of the museum? Really? You are going to try to tell me lies now?" Kat leaned in closer. "I've known you for more than a thousand years. I know something is not right with you. But know this—if you screw up, I will make your immortal life a living hell. You will have no more allies."

Ariadne gave a tired sigh. "What are you doing here, Kat? Are you following me?"

Kat's laugh rang with delight. "No, but that's not a bad idea. You need a little supervision. We would hate to have you stray."

Ariadne dropped her hands and ran her finger down the edge of the linen napkin. Her anger flared right beneath the surface, but Kat, the staff bearer, was the last person she could go against. "I'm not going anywhere."

"I'm glad to hear it." Kat waved at a passing waiter and pointed at the table. "Three cappuccinos."

The waiter nodded and walked toward the kitchen.

Ariadne glared at Kat. "Are you thirsty?"

"Not especially, but Tammy Blithe is on her way to meet me… well, us."

"Tammy. The witch?"

"One and the same. She and I were planning on going over the final plans for the ceremony. You will play your usual role, but this year I was hoping for more of an edge. We need to pay homage to Epione in a way only we can…" Kat stared at her.

Ariadne tried to ignore Kat's prompt, but after a minute of her piercing stare, she couldn't hold back any longer. "What do you want me to do?"

"Ah, well…you might not like it."

Of course I won't. Not if Kat is behind the idea.

Ariadne played with the napkin. "Just get it over with."

Kat smiled gleefully. "You may need to toughen your feet."

"What are you talking about?"

The waiter walked up with the tray of drinks. "Hello, ladies," he said with a smile, obviously unaware of the interruption.

Kat leaned into the man as he sat down the drinks.

"Oh, hello…" Reaching up, she ran her finger over his nametag, making the dark-haired man blush. "Giorgos."

He smiled. "Hey."

Kat looked into his eyes and smiled. "Giorgos," she crooned, "do you have a lover?"

He looked dazed with her intent stare. "A girlfriend."

Kat's smile never wavered. "Do you love her?"

"Yes. I think."

"You think? Does that mean you aren't sure?" Kat touched his hand.

"Yes…no…," the man stuttered. "I mean…you're so beautiful."

Kat dropped her fingers from his hand and ran them through her hair. "Thank you."

The waiter blinked a few times. "Uh, do you ladies need anything else?"

"Yes. I'm going to need you to come to me tonight." She pulled a card from her purse and slipped it into the breast pocket of his shirt.

"Definitely…," the man muttered.

"Excuse me, young man," a gray-haired woman said as she pushed her way around the waiter.

A small man stood at the woman's side, his head barely as high as the witch's waist. His skin was a mottled pale white, as if he had been covered in makeup. He pulled at his shirt collar and itched at his skin, and Ariadne caught a glimpse of a patch of gray skin under the edge of his shirt. He must be an elf. It had been a long time since she had seen one.

The waiter looked down at the little man.

"You may go." Kat directed him with a wave.

The gray-haired woman's eyebrows rose as the man spun on his heel and walked away. He looked back over his shoulder and his tray banged against the door that led inside.

"Well, you seem to be doing well." The woman chuckled. "By the way, this is my friend and assistant, Ivan Chenikylo."

The elf dropped his chin, in what she assumed to be a greeting.

"Nice to meet you, Mr. Chenikylo." Ariadne offered her hand.

He didn't move. "You can call me Ivan," he said in a thick Russian accent.

Ariadne dropped her hand. "Okay. Ivan."

Kat leaned back in her chair and looked down her nose. "I don't know why you even try. He's an elf, for the goddess' sake."

"Ya won't talk to my friend that way, Kat," Tammy growled. "Elf or not, you treat him with respect or ya will be finding yourself another witch."

"As always, Tammy, you know how to cause a commotion. Just keep your elf out of my way." Kat glared at the little man.

"I think y'all find that he's the best man you can get to protect your behind." The witch pulled out the extra chair and sat down. Ivan kept an eye on Kat as he silently moved around to the witch's side and pulled out the chair between her and Ariadne.

"Tammy, this is Ariadne Papadakis, one of the women from my group. She'll be in charge of the statue and the sacrifice."

"Ariadne? As in the daughter of King Minos? I've heard so much 'bout ya."

"She's one and the same," Kat said.

Ariadne nodded.

"Can't the poor lady answer for herself?" Tammy scoffed. The witch turned toward her with her back to Kat. "Aria, do you mind if I call you Aria? You can go on and call me Tammy. It's nice to finally put a name to the face."

"Yes, it's nice to finally meet. I've heard so much about you."

"All lies," Tammy said with a chuckle. "Though that one about Nico…that story's true. I skewered his big behind." The witch winked. "And if I get my say, Stavros will have a long and painful death just like his fat, piggy brother."

Ivan laughed, his sound low and menacing.

The waiter returned with three steaming cappuccinos. He took his time as he set down the cups, one in front of the witch, the elf, and Kat. His eyes never strayed from Kat's overly perky breasts.

Ariadne's hands clenched tight around the coffee cup in front of her. "Stavros told me about Nico." Ariadne paused, unsure if she should congratulate the woman, or hate her for killing Nico and wanting to kill Stavros.

Nico had always been known for his playboy behavior and his lack of settling his debts. Stavros had always cleaned up his brother's messes, and it had been a source of contention between her and Stavros. But, like any story, there had to be two sides. "What did Nico do to make you that angry?"

"Greek men are like dogs, they are always grumbling when they don't get their way. Nico couldn't handle a cat speaking her mind about what a fool he was; so he killed my teacher, the leader of my Coven, Angelica…" Tammy raised her hand in each direction. "Blessed be." She dropped her hand down into her lap and smiled wickedly. "Can't say I'm real sorry about ridding the world of him. This old alley cat still has a little bite left in her."

Ariadne's laughter echoed through the sparsely populated courtyard.

"While you have been in hiding, we've been busy," Kat said, interrupting.

Tammy looked back at Kat. "I wasn't hiding…I was just on a lengthy vacation."

Kat's eyebrow rose slightly. "A lengthy vacation involving killing, stealing, learning spiritualism, and hiring the elf, Ivan, to do your dirty work?"

"We all relax in our own ways, I suppose… But it is real sweet, you've been checking up on me. You're gonna make me blush."

Kat rolled her eyes with a huff. "I can't believe I had to resort to working with you."

Tammy smirked. "Ya were lucky I needed a bit of extra cash."

Ariadne turned just in time to watch as Ivan's coffee cup slipped from his fingers. He tried to catch it, but missed and the sound of glass breaking echoed through the almost empty courtyard surrounding the café.

Ivan bent over and started to pick up the chunks of glass dripping with coffee. "Shit."

Tammy dropped down to her knees and Ariadne followed. She scooped a bit of the glass together into a little pile. When she reached up to the table for a napkin, a pained "ouch" sounded from beneath the mesh table.

Tammy sat up. "Stupid glass, I shoulda known better." She held out her hand, where a long gash ran down the length of her finger. "I'm such a klutz sometimes."

Ariadne wrapped the napkin around the witch's finger and held it there to stop the bleeding. Tammy looked up and stared at her. "I once heard your sisterhood was able to heal. Can you fix this?"

Her question sounded more like an interview rather than a plea for help. Ariadne looked over to Kat, who was busy eyeing a passing man. She looked back to Tammy and leaned in so she could whisper. "We used to be able to heal, when our goddess was with us. But now all we have is our shift and our seduction. Sorry."

Tammy grabbed the napkin from Ariadne and squeezed. "Ah, don't be worrying, I can fix this right up. I was just wondering."

She and Tammy sat back up at the table. Ivan scooped the last bit of glass up, piled it in his napkin and sat it to the side. Tammy took a long swig of the coffee, plunked the cup down on the table and stared back at Ariadne with her almond-shaped, golden eyes. "Now ya never told me, how'd ya get yourself roped up under this one?" She pointed back at Kat.

Ariadne snickered. "I guess I'm just lucky."

"Ha! Real lucky." Tammy slapped her leg. "If ya are working under this one, you and me, we need to talk."

Kat glared at the witch. "The only thing Ariadne needs to worry about is the job I've given her."

Chapter Six

The black phone sat on Beau's desk next to his worn leather wallet. Should he call Stavros and let him know about the tablet? The governor had said he wanted to be notified if anything of importance was found. On the other hand, the tablet could be nothing—or it could be exactly what he had been looking for.

The morning light filtered into the room and made a bright line across the foot of the bed, where Kaden lay with his face down on the pillow.

He spun the little black rectangular object and watched it slowly come to a stop. Reaching over, he grabbed his thin wallet and pulled the dusty card from behind his ID. Flipping open the phone, he punched in the numbers and held his breath. He didn't need someone else to answer to, but it was better to have the authority on his side—even if the "authority" was an asshole.

"Governor Kakos' office, Bunny speaking," a perky voice answered.

"Hello, Bunny." *What kind of name is "Bunny?"* "This is Dr. Morris."

"Oh, Beau, yes, we met the other day. How can I help you?"

Then he remembered the blonde that had tagged along at Stavros' elbow. *Bunny, huh? Well, now it made a little more sense.*

"Well, my team and I just a made a small discovery I thought Governor Kakos needed to be informed of."

"Here, let me transfer you."

"No…wait." But the other end of the line was already taken by Greek elevator music. He groaned.

"Hello, Dr. Morris. So glad you called." He could hear the governor's fake smile through the phone line.

"Yes. Well you requested that I inform you of any interesting finds."

The governor cleared his throat. "Ah, yes. What did you come across?"

"It's nothing too incredible, just a tablet with some early Greek writing and a painting. It might turn out to be nothing. It's too early to know."

Beau refused to mention the inscription or the possible petroglyph of the Labyrinth. The governor would snoop around again if he thought there was anything of real value, and Beau couldn't afford to lose any more time.

"That sounds intriguing. Maybe I will have to come down and take a look."

"No," Beau said with a jerk. "I mean no, it's really nothing that you need to take time out of your busy schedule to come see."

"Hmm…then I'll just send down one of the news reporters. We need to create a buzz. This might be a good start—"

"No," Beau interrupted.

"I'll give them a call," the governor continued. "They should be down there sometime either today or tomorrow. I'll see what I can do. Hey, thanks for calling."

"Yeah," Beau groaned. *Great, more to deal with.*

The line went dead and Beau clicked his phone shut.

Kaden rolled over and pushed his black hair out of his eyes. "Everything okay?" he asked his voice still groggy.

Beau forced a smile. "Nothing for you to be worried about."

This is a burden only I can carry.

*

Vickie was on the other side of the dig, wearing a lower cut shirt than usual. Beau tried to divert his gaze, but with so much skin exposed it was hard not to notice.

"Hey, professor," one of the male students called. "I'm done here." He pointed at his square unit. "I'm gonna go over to dig four, okay?"

Of course the kid would want in dig four, Vickie's unit.

Beau nodded. "Go ahead."

Maybe this would be a good thing. At the very least, it would get Vickie's attention away from him for a while. Maybe she just needed a man's attention.

Beau looked over his notebook. He needed to get someone to translate Linear A. He had emailed a picture of it to Professor Ryan, but of course the man hadn't responded. He could visit the museum in Heraklion, but that meant seeing Ariadne again. And a man only had so much willpower.

He tapped his finger against his notebook as he thought.

"Beau, you need to call her," Kaden said with an exasperated sigh, as if he could read Beau's mind.

Beau looked over at him and stopped thumping. "What are you talking about?"

"You've been acting all…uptight. You need to make a move."

God, he hoped the kid was talking about Ariadne and not Vickie.

"On who?"

Kaden rolled his eyes. "That lady from the museum. You know…what's her name."

"You mean Ariadne Papadakis?"

"Yeah, that's right…Ariadne." Kaden smirked.

Since when did his son know how to manipulate him? He must've learned it from Lynda.

"I guess we'll see. I have a lot of work to do," he said as he flipped his notebook closed. "Where's Trina today? How come she's not around?"

Kaden shrugged and shoved the tip of the trowel into the soil. "She said she was busy."

"Uh oh, trouble in paradise?" The moment the words slipped out of his mouth, Beau felt guilty. The poor kid didn't need his old man to pry into his personal life.

Stabbing the ground again, Kaden grumbled something unintelligible.

"Sorry, kid. She seemed like a nice girl."

Pulling the tip of the trowel from the ground, Kaden frowned and looked up at him with a look of confusion on his face.

"She wasn't a nice girl?" Oh God, when he was a late teen he would have killed for that kind of girl.

"No, she's nice…she's just complicated."

"You've lived with your mother how long, and you are just figuring this out?" Beau laughed as he tossed his notebook on top of his bucket.

There was the crunch of tires on the gravel beside the unit. Beau stood up and walked to the crumbling sides of the pit. Peering out from the depths he made out the white high-heel sandal, his gaze flickered up the long tanned leg to the bottom of the wrinkled yellow sundress.

Beau couldn't find words. What was Ariadne doing here? She looked so beautiful, even more so than the day he'd met her.

The woman cleared her throat. "It's nice to see you again, Beau."

"Hey." He wiped the sweat from his hands against his pants leg.

She looked over at Kaden, "Hi, Kaden. I'm glad you're out here keeping your dad company."

Kaden looked at Beau with a guilty grin. "Yeah, he needs company."

Ariadne's laughter filled the uncomfortable silence. "I got a call that you had found something. May I see it?"

Was that the only reason she had come to see him? Just to see the tablet? In an unexpected way, he felt deflated, and the revelation surprised him. Did he really expect her to have come for any other reason than to inspect the find?

"Um, sure I guess," he stepped up and out of the pit and dusted off his pants with a slap.

"That's great." Ariadne played with the straps of her purse. "Sorry Kaden, I'll have him right back to you."

Kaden beamed. "Keep him as long as you want."

Beau turned away to hide his warm cheeks. It felt awkward as he led her in the direction of the bagged catalog under the tent. "Who told you about the find?"

She flipped her shiny hair over her shoulder with a twitch. "Stavros called me and said I needed to come down."

"You are on a first name basis with the governor?"

Her cheeks flushed. "Yes, he and I…I meant to say Governor Kakos. Governor Kakos is one of the museum's benefactors."

She glanced around, it was as if she was nervous or something. Jealousy flickered inside of him, but he tried to ignore it—she wasn't his.

The tent dimmed the unrelenting island sun, but the heat in the shade was as sweltering as it had been out in the dig, or it could have been the proximity to the beautiful woman. He grabbed the plastic bin and pulled it out from under the folding table. She stepped closer, and his heart beat faster. A light breeze brought an aroma of flowers and citrus from her glistening flesh.

She smells so damn good.

Looking up, he caught her golden eyes as she stared at him, but she quickly looked away.

He could have sworn that there had been something that had flickered between them, but he couldn't be sure. The last time he'd felt this way was when he had met Lynda.

He was such a mess.

Opening the box, he stared down at the clay tablet, the fresco of the woman stared back up at him. The woman's hair, though it was painted long ago, was the same shade of reddish brown as Ariadne's. The woman's nose was the same tiny thing with a slight curve to the tip.

"Wait, let me put on my gloves," Ariadne said, opening her purse as she pulled out a pair of blue latex gloves.

"Ah, don't worry about it. It's just a tablet. I just need someone to decipher it for me."

"I might be able to help." She leaned over and her hair brushed against his arm and made goose bumps rise on his skin. Reaching past him, her arm touched his and his heart pounded in his chest.

Pulling out the tablet, her eyes widened and her jaw dropped. "Where did you find this?"

"Where Kaden and I are working, dig three, in front of the column. I think it might be important, but I can't be sure. I mean, look at this." He pointed to the concentric circles.

She looked at him and frowned. "What are you hoping it means?"

Why wasn't she happy? Didn't she understand the implications? If he found the Labyrinth, it had the potential to change the course of history and right the wrongs of academics who refuted the existence of the Labyrinth. And it would forever place him in the history books as the man who unearthed a treasure trove of knowledge. He could leave Kaden a legacy the kid would be proud of.

Beau ran his hand over the back of his neck. "I hope I can find what I'm looking for."

"Mr. Morris, the Labyrinth is a myth."

He looked up and her face was filled with pity.

She thinks I'm crazy, just like everyone else.

The one person he had hoped would think he wasn't nuts was now just like all the rest who didn't believe in him. He would prove them—and her—wrong.

"That's what they said about Troy, that it was a myth. But I understand you're in the business of proof over conjecture." Beau looked out to the site where his students diligently sifted and scraped; they would find something she would have to believe in.

Ariadne smiled. "That's called science and it's what separates us from fantasy."

She was right, but it infuriated him that she was so dismissive of his dream. But then again, why should it matter to her? Why did he care so much if she cared? Her opinion was just that, an opinion.

"This script is interesting though," she paused.

He looked back at her and there was a light in her eyes. Was it hope?

"It talks about an ancient race and the story of Ariadne and the Minotaur. It looks like it's about the Labyrinth, like you hoped, but I think it's just an account of the ancient myth about Theseus and the bull, and how Ariadne gave him the golden thread."

Beau stared at the tablet. There had to be something more for it to tell. "Don't you think it means something that we found this in the era when the 'myth' was made?"

Ariadne shrugged. "Perhaps, but all stories begin somewhere."

There was the crunch of footsteps. The tent flap opened and Vickie appeared in the opening. "Hi, Beau…" she said with a velvet voice.

"Hello, Vickie. Can I help you?"

Vickie's eyes drifted to Ariadne. "Hi, I'm Vickie. One of Beau's…" she quickly glanced back at him, "*students*." The word fouled the tent with its tainted undertone of nastiness.

She pushed the tablet back into the box and balled her fists. "Vickie, this is Ms. Papadakis, she is the curator at the Heraklion Museum." He motioned toward Ariadne. "I'm sorry, is it Miss or Mrs.?"

Ariadne smiled. "Miss is fine."

Vickie's rigid posture softened. "Oh." She stuck out her hand. "Then it's nice to meet you."

Ariadne nodded, but said nothing.

"Vickie, did you need something?" Beau asked, breaking the strained silence in the tent.

For a moment, the girl looked confused. "Oh, never mind. I don't remember. I'll come back when I do." She gave Ariadne one more look and then stepped out with a quick backward wave.

He breathed a sigh of relief. "I'm sorry about that."

"No, don't worry. It's nice that your *students* check up on you."

The way she said the word made it clear that she too had heard the pronouncement. He grabbed the lid of the bucket and flipped it back on; but in his haste, he pushed it too far and the plastic lid clattered to the ground, forcing him to start again. Ariadne tried to stifle a giggle.

His cheeks felt like they were on fire, and he took a moment as he fastened the lid to let them cool.

When he stood up, she was watching him with a tiny smirk. "Do you mind if I go and see Kaden before I leave? I have something for him."

Pushing open the tent flap, he let her lead the way out. She bent over slightly and he could just make out the line created by her panties. He knew he shouldn't stare, but he couldn't tear his eyes away until she looked back over her shoulder. Hopefully she hadn't caught him staring, the day had already been enough of an embarrassment.

A blonde head bobbed next to Kaden as they approached. Trina looked up. "Hey, Ariadne. I didn't know you would be here."

Beau stared at Ariadne, who had a pinched look on her face. "What are you doing here, Trina?"

Trina pointed at Kaden. "Have you met my boyfriend?"

Kaden's face turned a vibrant red.

Ariadne frowned. "We've met."

"What did the tablet say, Beau?" Kaden asked, oblivious to the mysterious strain between the two women.

Beau stepped next to Ariadne. "Just a myth about the Labyrinth. I sent a picture off to Professor Ryan. Maybe he'll see some value in it. But it looks like it's probably not what we were hoping for."

Kaden shoved the tip of the trowel into the ground. "Sorry." He pulled the trowel and where the tip had been, a white surface lay exposed.

"What's that?" Beau said. He jumped down and took the trowel from Kaden.

He gingerly scraped away the soil. Lying exposed was a tiny bone. He cleared the soil around it, careful not to disturb the infant-sized femur. He looked up at Ariadne. "Oh, shit."

Chapter Seven

The tent filled with a flood of voices and the musky scents of the news broadcasters' colognes as everyone waited for Stavros to make a statement. Stavros milled around the crowd and warmed palms as the assortment of reporters pushed business cards into his pocket.

Beau stepped beside her and put his hand on her elbow. Ariadne looked down at his surprisingly familiar touch and smiled. The sweet touch felt so strange, but so wonderful at the same time. With Stavros there had never been touches, only nudges when he wanted sex or the formal handholding at political functions.

"Thanks for coming. It's nice to see someone I like," Beau said with a grin.

"I couldn't miss this," she said with a forced smile. *Kat had made sure of it.*

Beau dropped his hand as Vickie entered the tent and threw her hair behind her shoulder and extended her chest, making her breasts look like two smashed grapefruit under her V-neck top. Ariadne couldn't hold back her snicker. The girl was mistaken if she thought that Ariadne would stand in her way with Beau. Beau was sweet, good-looking, and ambitious, but there wasn't a possibility that they would be anything more than secret enemies.

Vickie walked up to them. "Hello again, Ariadne."

She nodded a welcome. "Vickie."

Beau shoved his hands in his pockets. "I hope the governor gets started soon, it's getting hot in here."

Stavros stepped next to her. "Hello, everyone. This is sure to gain headlines, don't you think?" He leaned in and gave Ariadne a kiss on her cheek. "It's a good day to be Greek."

Her gaze snapped to Stavros and she glared and silently reprimanded him for touching her. The bastard had no business with her anymore. They were through, but maybe that hadn't penetrated the man's ego.

Beau extended his hand to Stavros, but his eyes bore into her. "Governor."

The crowd seemed to tighten and a man bumped into her and smiled. "Sorry, Miss."

She nodded, but she couldn't stand being this close to so many people; especially not when the crowd included Stavros. Ariadne smiled at Beau. "I'm going to step out."

"I'll follow you out," Vickie said, motioning her to lead the way.

Ariadne smiled, but looked quizzically at Beau, who shrugged. "Uh, sure."

Beau reached out like he wanted to hold her back, but he stopped and looked at Stavros. His cheeks flushed. "Okay. See you in a bit."

The tent flap closed behind them and deadened some of the drone of the chatter. Kat and Tammy were perched on the wall at the far end of the site. Tammy's hands were flying as if she tried to desperately express a point she had made.

Vickie followed her away from the tent and out of hearing distance of the reporters. "What do you think is going to happen today?"

"I don't really know. Why?" She looked over her shoulder at Kat.

"I heard someone saying they thought the governor's going to shut us down. That can't happen. Beau will be devastated," the girl gushed.

Ariadne held back a smile. "Well, it's possible. They will need to do an investigation to make sure the body isn't a murder. Then there will need to be repatriation. And you know the Greeks like their ceremonies… They'll need to bury the body."

"Are you sure that the governor will close us down?" The lusty college student squirmed.

Ariadne shrugged. She could only hope that Stavros had finally realized what the dig could cost them.

"I need to go." Ariadne pointed at Tammy. "My friends are waiting."

"Sure." Vickie crossed her arms and bit nervously at her nails.

Kat's voices grew louder as she approached. "You can't stop it…" Kat turned away from Tammy. "Ariadne, have you talked to Stavros yet?"

"He'll come through."

"I hope you're right. I heard about the tablet. And the bones," Kat said.

"The dig is shut down."

"For now…but how long do you think Stavros is going to keep his cash flow stemmed? He's going to push the documents—for the body—through as fast as he can. Time is money."

"Hi, Tammy, it's nice to see you again." Ariadne ignored Kat's provocation.

"Howdy," Tammy answered with a wave. Her eyes were tired, and she looked relieved to have someone else besides Kat for company.

"Where's your assistant Ivan?" Ariadne asked as she looked around for the little gray-skinned elf.

"Oh, he had some business calling him. He'll be along sometime, I'm sure," Tammy said, her gaze flashed to Kat, then down at the ground.

It seemed out of character for the woman to be subordinate to Kat. What was going on?

"You okay, Tammy?" She looked over at Kat, who had a wicked smile on her face.

"She's fine." Kat answered for the witch. "Aren't you?"

"Yeah, I'm fine. Really." Tammy looked over at the tent. "I'm just getting nervous 'bout the ceremony. That's all."

Ariadne didn't believe her, but there was no point in pressing the issue. "Are you guys ready for the ceremony? Did you get everything you needed?"

"We still need a goat, then we'll be all set," Tammy said with a sigh. "Are you thinking you'll be bringing Stavros?"

Kat glared at Tammy.

Ariadne sighed. "I don't think so."

"Do you care for Stavros?" Tammy asked as Kat continued to stare daggers at her.

Ariadne thought for a moment. "To be honest…I think he's a bastard. I wish I would've left him years ago."

"I glad to hear ya say that," Tammy said with a wide smile. "I like you. To see you with a man like Stavros…it's a shame. You gotta spark the rest of us drool after."

Kat snickered. "You don't know her very well. She's lived more than a thousand years. If she was *great* don't you think she would've done something *great* by now?"

Ariadne gritted her teeth. *She has no idea what I'm capable of, one of these days she'll be shocked…but then again, I've been saying that for so long.* She sighed. *Nothing's ever going to change.*

Tammy glared at Kat. "It's a cruel joke that the gods made you such a power-hungry harlot and her such a meek soul. But the gods always have a way of making things right."

"Ariadne already wasted her chance at becoming great when she ostracized herself from the god Dionysus. He pitied her and offered her his hand, but she couldn't handle his infidelities—I think she couldn't please him." Kat smirked. "Hadn't you heard about her fall from grace?"

Ariadne's cheeks flushed, and a thin veil of sweat covered her forehead. "Stop it."

"What did you say?" Kat snarled. "Don't think that because you finally have someone who feels sorry for you, that you can stand up to me. That's a battle you will lose… Or are you trying to hide the truth of your past from your little ally?"

A squeal of a microphone came from the tent. "Ladies and gentlemen, we would like to present to you our beloved, honorable Governor Kakos!" A round of applause followed.

"Let's go," Kat ordered. Standing up, she sauntered off ahead of them.

"I'm sorry," Tammy said. "Ya need to find your tongue and use it to lash that woman down."

"Katarina saved our most sacred relic from being destroyed. She holds a high esteem within our sisterhood. If I go against her, it would be like going against everything we hold sacred. I would be going against all my sisters."

"She ain't without flaw." Tammy smirked. "And just because she did one great thing, doesn't mean that ya don't get to stand up for yourself or what ya believe in."

While Ariadne had been talking, someone had rolled up the sides of the tent, allowing the ocean breeze to clear the scents of the mass of people. Beau's equipment had been removed and in its place were white folding chairs and a water cooler for the reporters who filled the seats. Kat led the way into the tent and forced her way into the farthest corner from Stavros, who stood behind the makeshift podium at the front of the tent.

Bunny sat in a seat in the back, far removed from the man who Ariadne had seen standing between the woman's thighs. Stavros tilted his head in greeting, but she pretended to ignore the gesture and instead took a seat next to a handsome young reporter, right behind Kat.

"Thank you all for coming," Stavros started. "As you all know, Crete is the greatest place on earth. We are blessed with agricultural richness, bountiful marine life, and the most beautiful women." The crowd laughed.

His charm was magnetic and his charisma undeniable. Watching him in action as he worked the crowd reminded her why she had dated the man for so many years. He had many public qualities that made him a fine catch, but she could never forgive him for all the wrongs he had inflicted. He was no different from any of the men of her past.

A warm hand touched her shoulder and she jerked.

"Is he always like this when he speaks?" Beau whispered into her ear.

She smiled when she looked up and saw her rescuer. "Yes. He's a politician."

"Well, he's good." Beau growled. "Did he tell you what he's planning?"

Her guilt gnawed at her when she looked at Beau's handsome face. He didn't deserve what they were doing to him…no, what *she* was doing to him. If only he'd chosen a different location…she would not have been forced to stop him.

"I'm so sorry—"

"It sounds like he wants to bring in tourists who will pay to take part in the dig," he interrupted. "He's gonna try to get a bunch of slobbering yuppies to shovel in my site."

"What?" Ariadne whispered, her gaze flashed toward the blabbering politician.

"I was afraid they'd shut down the site for repatriation and burial of the body, but it sounds like he wants to just keep going. He said he found a private group of citizens who want to bury the remains."

He looked relieved, but Ariadne's heart sank. What was Kat going to say?

"This's going to save me thousands, but cost me my reputation, and probably destroy the site." He dropped his hand as he stood up. Where Beau's moist breath had warmed her ear, suddenly turned cold.

Ariadne stared at the man, as she tried to keep the fears that fluttered in her chest from leaking out onto her face. Stavros wouldn't compromise everything to make money, would he?

Stavros' voice broke through the fog in her mind. "…after much deliberation we, Beau Morris and I, have decided to open this dig up for the public to participate…"

Her heart fell to the ground. There would be no stopping it now.

Kat turned around. "I thought you said you had this handled," she hissed.

"I…he…promised me…" Ariadne stammered.

Kat glared at her. "You'll never change. I knew I couldn't depend on you."

An explosive roar tore through the tent.

At the sound of the gunshot, Ariadne threw her body to the ground. People screamed, chairs banged against each other, and the microphone popped and emitted an ear-piercing squeal. Beau reached out and took her hand. Grabbing her other arm, he pulled her toward him and took her in his embrace.

"Are you okay?" he yelled above the jumble of noise.

People frantically scurried around them. She looked into his brown eyes. There was strength in them she had never noticed before. For a moment, she could say nothing. She could only look at the man whose arms were wrapped around her.

"Where's Kaden?" Ariadne looked behind him, but she couldn't see the young man anywhere.

Beau's heavy breath poured onto her face. "He's with Trina."

Relief filled her. Beau and Kaden were okay.

A woman screamed. "The governor! He's been shot!"

Stavros stood up on a chair at the front of the tent. He held his neck as blood ran through his fingers and down the front of his suit jacket. "Don't worry. I'm fine. Just a little flesh wound."

"Get down!" Beau yelled at Stavros.

Stavros clamored down from the chair. At least he had the sense to listen for once in his life.

Beau looked at her. "Are you going to be okay?"

She nodded.

Without warning, he leaned in and took her mouth with his. She closed her eyes and let the warmth of his lips spread into her soul. His strong hand rubbed the space between her shoulders; the simple motion comforted her like nothing she had ever felt.

As quickly as he had taken her, he pulled back. "I…I'm sorry…," he stuttered. "I just… You're—"

She pressed her finger to his lip and silenced him. "Don't worry, Beau. I understand this—you needed to know you're alive."

"No—" he began, but again she stopped him.

"Don't apologize." She pressed her hands against his chest. His eyes were wide and his mouth agape as she moved out of his arms.

A part of her wanted to stay there and be surrounded by his wanting touch, but it wasn't right. Her loyalty was with her sisterhood, and she couldn't be seen with their enemy.

A thought struck her, he was their enemy, but could he be a lover? If they never went public. If they kept their affair in the shadows, maybe…

No… When his lips had pressed against hers, the feelings that ran between them were not that of simple lust. And more than lust was an emotional risk she wasn't willing to take. She could have sex with anyone, but not a man with whom there was a possibility of something more than a physical connection.

She tried to push the thoughts of more from her mind. There were too many reasons they couldn't be together.

Beau stood up and looked around. The people that were still left in the tent were sprawled on the ground at his feet. He looked god-like the way he scanned the horizon for danger. Reaching down, he pulled a phone from his back pocket and flipped it open. "We're going to need an ambulance."

*

The pungent scent of antiseptic mixed with the stale scent of the sick as Ariadne walked down the hospital's long white corridor. Some of the people's doors were open as if they awaited people who would hopefully come. Other doors were shut, but the sounds of moaning escaped beneath the thin cracks and invaded the still hall.

Stavros's room was easy to find by the crowd who stood outside the door. The group talked in hushed voices as she approached. Bunny stood at the group's center, her face pale and mascara ran down her cheeks. The woman looked up at her and smiled weakly. "Ariadne, I'm glad you're here…"

If Bunny had said she married the prime minister of Britain, Ariadne couldn't have been more shocked. The woman, who she had only seen days before naked beneath Stavros, now wanted to be kind and welcoming to her?

Ariadne looked around the crowd of faces surrounding the governor's mistress. A dark-haired man with stubble and pockmarked face stood at Bunny's left, and Ariadne recognized him as Christos, the head of Crete's Hellenic Police from the dinners she had spent with the governor. Behind him, stood a man with a camera slung around his neck. Bunny's gaze flickered to the man with the camera. Bunny must have noticed and she stepped toward Ariadne and opened her arms and motioned for a hug.

The photographer picked up his camera, but Ariadne couldn't bring herself to play the game. The thought of playing the former lover was too much. She couldn't choke down the thought of people pitying her while inwardly they likely wondered if she had something to do with the assassination attempt.

She should've never come here. Then again, if she hadn't, the rumors would've been even more virulent. Crete was a small island filled with big mouths and even stronger opinions.

Ariadne smiled at Christos and offered her hand, ignoring Bunny's outstretched arms. "Nice to see you, Christos. Any leads yet?"

Bunny's arms dropped.

Christos shook her hand. "I can't believe what has happened. There's been talk about some conflicting feelings from underground groups about Stavros' politics, but none of the rebels or protestors has the funds to pull off this type of thing."

Rebels…it was possible that civil unrest could have been the reasoning behind the shooting, but it didn't seem to fit. Why would rebels wait until he was at the archeological dig to shoot him? Stavros made many public appearances with much larger crowds. If they wanted to send a message, one of his larger addresses would have seemed like the more logical location. But then again, rebels could've seen this as an opportunity to get closer to him; he didn't have as large of an entourage, or as many security officers.

Christos stared at her, as if he was looking for clues. "I heard you and Stavros recently ended your affair. Yes?"

Looking over at Bunny's smeared mascara, Ariadne nodded. "It was time."

"Neither of you had hard feelings?" Christos pressed.

Ariadne looked at his broad nose. As he breathed, a hair from his nose vibrated and squirmed as it tried to escape. "Christos, if I didn't care for Stavros, do you think I would be here?"

Christos glanced at the blonde and shrugged. "You make a point."

"Yes. Now, if you will excuse me." Without waiting for an answer, she pushed past the throng of people and opened the door.

Stavros was sitting up in bed with his eyes closed. His neck was wrapped in white gauze, spotted with brown-red blotches where the blood had oozed and then dried. His face was pale and though she had known him for thousands of years, this was the first time he had ever looked *old*.

Her heart clenched in her chest. She had never loved this man, but seeing him hurt and surrounded by people who would never know who he really was, she couldn't help the pity that rose within her. She was one of only a few that knew what a powerful and caring man Stavros could be. He had many faults, but he had cared for her for more years than she could remember. Maybe she was wrong to have ended things between them.

The door clicked shut behind her and he opened his eyes. Seeing her, he smiled tiredly. "Aria, you came."

"Hi, Stav. Flesh wound, eh?" she said, trying to lighten the thick air between them.

He patted the bandage on his neck. "I just needed a vacation, but they forced me to wear the bandage to keep people from calling me 'lazy.'"

"Ah, good idea. You want to make voters feel sorry for you." She looked over to the window, where floral arrangements were packed so tightly it looked as if a flower shop had exploded in the room. "Well, it looks like your little act is working."

His lips quivered with a smile.

She looked back over her shoulder at the closed door. "Stavros, I'm sorry."

He stared quizzically at her. "Why?"

"If I wouldn't have planted the bones, you wouldn't have been there. This wouldn't have happened."

"Aria, I've had a bounty on my head for a long time. This was bound to happen eventually." He sat up in bed and stretched out his back.

"And who knows," he continued with a strong, energetic voice. "Maybe this will bring an edge of intrigue to the island. There has to be some way to spin this to pick up the economy."

He will never change.

Stavros looked out the window. "Maybe I can start hiring more police. That would make more jobs. It would definitely be a great way to gain public opinion."

"Stavros, you know as well as I do that this site needs to be shut down."

A thin nurse walked into the room with a knock. Stavros dropped back into bed. "Hello?" he said in a weak voice, ignoring Ariadne's reminder.

The big fake.

"Oh, governor, how are you feeling?"

"Well, my back…"

"Let me get that for you." The busty nurse walked to the head of the bed and bent over to fluff the pillow behind Stavros' head.

His eyes wandered downward and Ariadne smiled. *Same old Stavros.*

Ariadne walked out the door without saying goodbye.

Bunny stood outside the room with fresh tears on her cheeks. "Is he doing any better? He's so weak."

Ariadne smiled. "He's weak all right."

Chapter Eight

"The police have shut down the site," Beau grumbled. He stuffed his hands into his pockets and leaned against the window frame.

Kaden flopped down on the bed with a squeak. "For how long?"

Beau shrugged. "Who the hell knows between the bones and the shooting? Could be a day, could be a coupla weeks."

Beau pushed off from the wall and went over to his computer on the tiny desk. He opened up the lid and clicked a few buttons, no emails, no messages, nothing. Slamming the lid shut, he walked back to the window. He had only been in the apartment for a few hours, yet the walls had already begun to move in on him.

He looked over at Kaden who had his hands under his head and his eyes closed. Beau couldn't help but feel angry with the boy. The kid just didn't understand what this meant. He had already lost days when he'd shown up on his doorstep and now he was losing an indefinite amount of time. Time was money and Kaden didn't even seem to understand or care.

Kaden pushed his ear buds into his ears and clicked on his MP3 player. Beau clenched his jaw. He needed to get out of the apartment.

"Kae, I want you to stay here. I'm going for a walk."

Kaden pulled out his ear buds. "What?"

"You stay. I'm going out," Beau growled.

"Trina and I were planning on meeting up later. Cool?"

"Yeah. Whatever. When are you planning on being home?" As soon as the words escaped his lips, he knew he had screwed up. This place wasn't his son's home. This place was about as far as the kid had ever been away from home. And there he went bringing it up, bringing up that his mother had left him with a father he had barely known.

Son of a bitch. He was never going to get this "father" thing down.

Kaden coughed, then pushed the ear buds back into his ears. "Later, Beau."

Beau grabbed his wallet. Stepping out the door, he looked back and watched his pale, black-haired son sitting alone on the worn rented bed. "You wanna come with me?"

Kaden gave him a dull, tired look. Beau stood there and waited for his son to answer, but Kaden only waved him off.

Stepping out the front door of the apartment building, a brown snake slithered off the doorstep and disappeared into a small green bush. The boy in him wanted to go after the snake and take it back to his son to see, but the man in him made him stop. His son didn't want him around. Kaden wanted to be left alone, and maybe things were easier that way.

He walked aimlessly down the streets. An elderly Greek woman wearing a long black dress and a black head cover came out of a shop. He waved out of habit and the old woman glared at him suspiciously. Saying something he couldn't understand, she turned her back on him and walked in the opposite direction. Even strangers were against him now.

He came to a street market where vendors called to him in Greek and waved at him to visit their tables. He walked from table to table as he inspected everything from fresh fish to leather wallets, but he bought nothing. He passed by a small bar, its windows were filmed with grease and soot and only a yellow light could be seen from the outside.

He kept walking. One merchant's table was covered in red, yellow, and green spices. Stopping, he leaned in and pulled in the earthy scents of the warm, freshly ground powders. In a strange way, they reminded him of Ariadne. It could've been their vibrant colors or the way they made his mouth water, but for a moment, he could think of nothing but the feel of her against his body.

He had screwed up with her. He should have never touched her. From the way the governor had kissed her, it was clear that she was spoken for.

Why had he let himself kiss her?

Now the one person he really knew and liked, besides his son and his crew, hated him. All because he couldn't control his damn urges. What was he, some teenager? Was being around Kaden and Trina beginning to rub off on him?

He didn't have time for a woman in his life, certainly not a woman who didn't want to have anything to do with him. He was too old to go chasing after someone.

And what will happen if Ariadne is a flake like Lynda? He shook his head. There was no way the beautiful brunette who ran the museum, was kind to a boy she didn't even know, and was willing to help a lackluster archeologist, was anything less than amazing.

The next stand was filled with fruit and vegetables, and the man behind the table was dark from the sun. "Whatchu need?"

He looked the surly guy in the eye. "To be honest, I need a little good luck. You got any of that?"

The dark-haired man stared down at him for a moment. All of a sudden, the beefy man chuckled. His body jiggled. "Don't we all?" The man picked up an apple and tossed it to him. "Here, this's the best I can do."

Beau nodded and lifted the apple. "Hey, it's a start. Thanks. How much do I owe you?"

The man laughed. "On the house. But when you find some luck, come back and find me."

Beau smiled. "Will do…"

He hadn't made it far when he saw a familiar brunette head and yellow sundress. Slung on her arm was a cotton bag with an orange flower poking over the edge. She was talking to a merchant, and he couldn't take his eyes off her. The way she smiled with her whole face made his heart shift in his chest. He had never noticed the way she talked with her hands, or the way she flipped her hair over her shoulder the moment before she laughed.

He walked toward her as if there was a magnet in his center that pulled him in her direction.

He stood behind her for a moment. "I'm glad to see you are okay."

God…I'm so suave…

Ariadne jerked. "What?" She turned away from the merchant and faced him. "Oh…hi, Beau."

His cheeks warmed. "I just said I was glad you were feeling okay. I mean after everything that happened. You know with the governor and everything. I was worried. I mean, I wasn't sure how you would take it. I mean… God, I'm sorry I'm yammering."

She smiled and there was a light in her eyes. "Don't worry about yammering, Beau. It's nice to see you. And I'm fine."

"Is the governor okay?"

Ariadne stared at him with her golden eyes as questions played across her face. "I think he'll recover."

He could skirt around the issue, but he needed to know the truth and put an end to the fluctuating emotions that were invading his life. "What's going on between you two?"

Her shoulders fell. "I was hoping you wouldn't ask."

"I'm sorry. It's none of my business…"

She stepped away from the merchant's stand. "Stavros and I've known each other a long time."

Beau's phone rang and its interruption came as a relief. Pulling the phone out of his pocket, he looked down at the caller ID, George Tramp, his contact at the NSF. He looked up at Ariadne. "Sorry, I have to answer this, but don't go anywhere."

She smiled and turned back to the vegetable merchant.

Beau walked around the corner, opened the phone and pressed it to his ear. "Hello, Dr. Morris speaking."

His heart raced. Hopefully George was calling him to let him know the grant had come through.

"Hello, Beau. This is Dr. Tramp, with the National Science Foundation."

"Yes? How can I help you?"

"Well, Beau, I'm calling to let you know that we were impressed with your last find…" There was a long pause. "However, I just received a call about the incident with Governor Kakos."

Oh shit…how did he find out so fast?

"Safety is our number one concern for those taking part in research we facilitate, safety not only for those in the field, but for those who are influenced by their work as well. As it stands, we have enormous concerns about your work."

No…no…no…

Beau gulped. "Well, sir, I can promise you that this was an isolated incident. I doubt that it had anything to do with our dig."

"Either way, we are worried about your safety."

Tramp had him backed into a corner. How was he going to get out?

He waited for the axe to fall.

"As such, I am sorry to inform you, but we will no longer be able to fund your work. And it may be in your and your team's best interests to return to the U.S. at the end of the month."

Two weeks. The phone slipped in Beau's hand. "Is there anything I can do to change your mind?"

Tramp sighed. "It would take an act of God. Beau…I'm sorry. I'll contact Professor Ryan and let him know."

The world around him went blurry and the sounds of the market were muffled. "Yeah…you're sorry…"

"Don't be afraid to come see me when you get back. Again, I'm sorry." The phone line went dead.

Beau's hand fell and he leaned back into the wall, next to a garbage can. The punches just wouldn't stop coming. Maybe it would be better to leave Crete, go back to the States, back to the school, and forget about this project. Cut his losses. The head of the college would have something to say, but what could he do? Fire him? Yeah…he could fire him all right.

Beau slid the phone in his pocket and clenched his eyes shut. *Why can't anything go right?*

"You okay?" Ariadne said, her voice cutting through the ringing in his ears.

He opened his eyes. Ariadne stared at him.

He couldn't say anything. What could he say? He had failed? He was a loser? He stared into her glittering eyes, and for a moment, reminded himself to breathe.

Ariadne smiled. "You do realize you are holding an apple in your hand, right?"

He looked down at the red orb he was clutching in his left hand. Funny he would ask for luck and life would hand him an apple—the symbol of evil temptation, failure, and disgrace.

Ariadne reached over and took the orb from his numb fingers. She stood up and smiled empathetically. "Are you hungry?"

He limply shook his head "no." Food was the furthest thing from his mind. He needed to find the Labyrinth, he needed to find a new grant—and both things would be damned hard to find in two weeks.

"Great, I'm starving." She took a bite of the red, corrupted apple. A drip slipped down the corner of her mouth and she brushed it away with the tips of her fingers.

The apple rolled from her hand and dropped into the garbage can with a thud. "What's going on with you, Beau? Aren't you happy about the site being opened to visitors?" she asked, but her voice was filled with a distinct edge of anger.

"Someone called the NSF."

"What?" she asked, as she wiped her fingers against the hem of her yellow sundress.

"They cut my funding."

Her gaze snapped up to his face as she dropped the edge of her dress. A smile flickered across her lips, but was quickly replaced by a look of concern. "What are you going to do?"

He looked at her golden eyes and let his gaze move down to her dirt-smudged shirt.

She hasn't changed since we'd been together in the tent...

He smiled, wild and menacing. "You know what, Aria? I'm gonna fight. I'm gonna fight 'til I find what I know is there. I'm gonna dig until my fingers bleed and I have no skin left on my knees. I'm going to change history."

Beau grabbed her hand and pulled her into the street. "Where are we going?" she asked, but allowed him to lead her without protest.

He didn't answer. Instead, he pushed through the crowds of people until he finally reached the small bar he had spotted.

Ariadne pulled back. "Let's go somewhere else. Trust me...The Mouse Hole isn't a great place for tourists."

Ignoring her, he put his hand on the door and pushed. The door opened with a loud creak and he pulled Ariadne inside. A table of ribald men looked up as they entered. The largest of the group looked past him and smiled at Ariadne with a mouth full of black teeth. The man ran his hands over his greasy hair, and Beau pulled Ariadne in the opposite direction. They had been through enough for one day; all they needed was a drink.

A big-chested woman stomped over to their table with a begrudging sigh. She bent over as she reached for the menus at the far side of the table, and her breasts threatened to spill over the thin fabric of her grease-stained top. Ten years earlier, the woman may have been considered attractive, but with a finger of gray in her almost-black hair mixed with the creases around her lips, she bordered on disturbing. The saying "ridden hard and put away wet" came to mind as he tried to look anywhere but at her over-tanned cracking chest, which rested in front of his face.

She thrust the menus into each of their hands. "Whatta ya want?" she grumbled.

Crete was known for their great wines, but from the flickering lights and the dank smell of urine that wafted around them, this bar didn't seem like the right place to order a Shiraz. "Ouzo, straight up."

The woman made a grumbling noise and looked at Ariadne. Ariadne shifted slightly in her seat. She turned the menu over in her hands and her tattoo came into view. The barkeep sucked in her breath. "I'm sorry, Mistress…I didn't recognize you." The woman wiped her dirty fingers on the thighs of her skirt, leaving a grimy trail in their wake.

Ariadne shook her head slightly. "We'll take two of those, in *regular* glasses."

The lady spun on her heel and almost sprinted back to the wooden bar.

"Regular glasses?" he asked, confused by what had just transpired.

She looked at him and smiled. "Yes. You don't want the ones they give the tourists."

She didn't need to say more. "Why'd she treat you like you're royalty?"

Just then, the waitress came back with two sparkling glasses filled to the lip with the clear ouzo. Setting down napkins, she gently placed the full glasses in front of them with a tiny bow. "These're on the house."

Ariadne nodded. As the woman turned, Beau noticed a small tattoo of a mouse on the woman's ankle. In a way, it was comical, a tiny little mouse on such a brusque woman. He looked over at Ariadne's arm, but the snake was covered—it was odd to be around two people with tattoos that in no way seemed to epitomize their personalities.

People were strange.

The man with the wide nose stared at him. Beau poured the ouzo into his mouth, and it was like a fire as it rippled down his throat. He held back the urge to cough.

The barkeep stomped over to the group of men at the other table, grabbed the empties and clanked them together. Turning away from the table, the man with an eye-patch slapped her on the ass and laughed. "You busy later?"

Beau pushed his chair away from the table, and began to rise, but Ariadne grabbed his hand and shook her head. The barkeeper laughed tiredly, as if the physical contact was nothing new, but it infuriated him. Even the tough-looking barkeep deserved a little respect.

Ariadne pushed his drink toward him and he slammed it back, banging it on the table as he brought it down.

Ariadne leaned toward him. "There's nothing you can do. Besides, she's tougher than she looks, the men won't get away with anything more."

The woman brought a bottle to the table and refilled Beau's glass. She wouldn't look him in the eyes. Was her aversion out of embarrassment or shame for the way the men had treated her?

His anger rose as he looked over at the men and noticed that the five of them were all glaring in their direction. "Assholes," he muttered.

"What was that?" the broad-nosed man said in a dangerous voice.

Beau forced himself to remain sitting, but he wanted to punch the ugly guy in the face. "I said *treat the woman with a little respect.*" He could only control one thing, his body or his tongue, and the tongue lost.

The lackeys turned and stared at the broad-nosed man as his eyes drew into angry slits. "You stupid Americans. You think you can come in here and tell me how to act?"

Beau couldn't stop himself. "Being American has nothing to do with knowing how to treat a woman."

Ariadne grasped his hand and squeezed. "Stop," she whispered.

She was right. It was unwise to act out with so many against him. He might be able to take one, but five was outside of his range of ability. When the site opened back up, he would need both his hands, and his ass. Damn his mouth.

The man's chair scraped on the floor as he stood up. He motioned for his friends to stay and he strode confidently to the edge of their table. He pressed his face close to Beau.

Beau could smell the scent of cheap liquor and the pungent odor of fish as it permeated from the man.

"Here in Crete, we don't appreciate your kind. You academics come here and bring in your unchecked little students. You steal our treasures and destroy our culture with your Western ways."

Beau stared at the man. "You have it all wrong. I'm trying to save your culture, not destroy it."

"That's why you come here and take our jobs, leaving us to find work off the island, or fish. You know what it's like to rely on fish for a living?" The man drove his finger into Beau's chest. "No… you don't have a clue."

Beau forced the man's finger from his chest. "If you think I'm getting rich by looking in the dirt for artifacts, you're dead wrong."

"Boys," the barkeeper said, stepping between them. "If you want to fight, take it outside."

The man glared at him. Turning, he walked back to his table as he muttered something under his breath in Greek.

"Don't worry about the rats," the barkeep said.

Ariadne motioned toward the man. "Why don't you take him your *special?*" Her voice had an icy edge. Ariadne reached into her grocery bag, but before she could get her wallet, Beau handed the woman his last twenty Euros.

Without another word, the woman strode off to the bar and grabbed a blue bottle from under the counter. She walked it over to the man's table and dropped it down with a thump. "Your friend over there wanted to buy you all a drink."

The men looked over at them and lifted their drinks slightly. "Thanks," the smaller man of the group grumbled in a thick Greek accent.

Ariadne smiled wickedly. "You're welcome."

The man leaned back to his friend. "See? I told you snakes and mice were nothing."

His friend nodded and said something back in Greek.

But what had the man meant when he said "snakes" were nothing? He was no snake and Ariadne, the curator, seemed far from dangerous.

As the afternoon wore on, they talked about the museum and their curating methods. He talked about his dig while he took gulps of clear liquor straight from the bottle. The alcohol that had burned on his lips, soon slid down with the ease of warmed milk. Ariadne's tanned cheeks took on a pink hue and a damp sheen wetted the skin around her lips.

A drip of sweat slipped down his chest as he leaned across the table toward Ariadne. She was so close he could smell the ouzo on her breath and the floral scent of her perfume, which made his heart thunder in his chest. "You know, you're stunning."

A crash interrupted his train of thought. He turned and watched the wide-nosed man fall to the floor. His friends stood up and circled around him, as if they were unsure of how to respond.

The barkeep cackled. "Take your boss and get out. If he can't hold his booze he shouldn't be in a bar."

The small man sneered and said something in slurred Greek. He looked over at Ariadne. "Messing with people like you… Governor Kakos deserved what he got."

The barkeeper glared at the man.

Ariadne's eyes were filled with anger and her jaw was clenched. "The governor is a far better man than any of you…if you had anything to do with the attack… I'll—"

"Ariadne," the barkeep interrupted with a warning glance. "Don't worry about these boys. It's just the rat poison talking."

The small man stared at the barkeeper, his face twitching with anger.

Beau's mind was filled with a fog, making everything blur together. Rat poison? He had paid for the man to be poisoned? He looked at Ariadne's blank face. Her edges were fuzzy and she looked so *soft*.

A poisoning softy. He laughed at his private joke.

In the back of his mind, he wondered if he should be upset with her actions, but instead he emptied his glass.

The other men stood up from the table and shifted the man on the floor back to his feet. "We'll be back. And you and your snake'll get what's comin'."

The barkeep gave him a sticky sweet smile. "We'll be waiting. And next time, I'll use a heavier hand. Or…I'll call Nico's former friend, Ms. Blithe. Not everyone gets to walk away from her *methods*."

The men fell silent and hurried out the door, half dragging their fallen superior.

The door slammed shut behind them. Ariadne lifted the bottle to her glass, but only drops fell from its edge. "Ah. It must be time to go."

"Where?" He stood up out of his chair and slid it back on the wooden floor. Emboldened by the liquor, he took her hand possessively and pulled her to standing. "Show me your island."

He stepped to her and pulled her into his arms even though her body was tense and hard. He didn't care. For once in his goddamned life, he didn't care. He needed this. He needed a moment of something good. And one kiss…one hurried, stupid, idiotic kiss hadn't been enough.

He leaned in and took her lips. Gripping the back of her dress, his fingers pressed into her back. Her eyes were wide and her lips rigid.

She reached up as if she would push him away, but she stopped. Her eyes closed. Her hand lowered to his shoulder and she relaxed inside of his arms.

Closing his eyes, he let the need he felt inside of him overflow the boundaries of right and wrong, of social customs, and business relationships. Her lips tasted sweet as his tongues passed over, gently flicking away the slight taste of the apple and the airy flavor of the ouzo.

She moaned into his mouth and her body pressed into him. *Yes…she wanted this too.*

Chapter Nine

The full moon's light reflected off the water and lit up the beach, where Ariadne's grocery bag had been dropped in their haste to reach the surf. A drooping orange flower fell out onto the sand, next to the heap of clothing they had left behind. The scrub brush-covered hills encompassed them in the tranquil bay. The waves splashed over their bodies as she relaxed to the sound of Beau's breath.

She had found a way to safely explore her feelings—his site was closed—he would surely be leaving soon. He had no reason to stay and a quick romance would be the cure for the feelings… no, the lust…they both clearly wanted to explore.

She ran her fingers over his glistening shoulder, leaving a trail of goose bumps in their wake.

There wouldn't be time for him to fall in love with her. He was safe from the curse—as long as he didn't love her. For once, she could go enjoy her life—at least for a moment. And after he left, she could look back on this one rebellious night.

Ariadne wrapped her arms tighter around Beau's shoulders. "I'm sorry about those men at the bar. I hate to fight."

"Don't worry about them. They were drunk…stupid." Beau's lips tickled the skin of her neck as her fingers ran up through his wet hair.

"This is my favorite beach. Private…" And none of her sisters would find them. They were all undoubtedly preparing their bodies for tomorrow night's festival.

Beau lifted his lips from her skin and glanced around the narrow inlet. "It's beautiful, but not as beautiful as you."

If he only knew that she had been the cause behind the closing of his site, he wouldn't have thought she was beautiful. He would hate her for the foul creature she was. Her stomach clenched with guilt, and the liquor swirled as it rose into her throat.

She tried to swallow her guilt away, but no reprieve came. She pressed her lips to his. Lightly, she flicked her tongue against his firm bottom lip. He tasted like the salty water and the burn of ouzo.

Her head was filled with blurred thoughts of reasons why she shouldn't be naked in his arms, but her need silenced her concerns.

The water ebbed from them, exposing her wet chest to the cool night air. Beau sucked in a breath and leaned down to her breasts. He took her nipple into his mouth and sucked lightly as he ran his warm hands down her waist. The touch made her burn with desire.

She could feel how badly he wanted this, her, here, now. She lifted his chin and pressed her lips against his. She nibbled his bottom lip until a moan rumbled from his lips.

Stavros was nothing like this; instead, he was always hurried in his lovemaking, thrusting and grunting like a rutting bull.

Beau nuzzled her neck and pulled at her ear with his teeth, making her body writhe. His fingers slid down her skin, stopped at the small of her back and moved her against him.

A wave crashed against them and pushed his body harder against her. He grasped her tighter. Even Poseidon wanted them to unite.

He looked up at her with his sexy brown eyes filled with a need mirrored by her body.

The water made his hands slide easily down to her legs, and he pulled them around him as their lips met. Their kiss was rushed, filled with a hunger that yearned to be satisfied, while his hands slid down her ass and his fingers found her. She gasped as his fingers moved inside of her tender, wanting flesh.

Reaching under the water, she ran her hand down his length. She moved her hand back up and swirled his tip in her palm. He moaned in her mouth and his fingers moved faster inside of her.

He was hot in her hand. Moving her hips, she led him inside of her. The heat of him filled her perfectly and let her body move with the motion of the waves. Beau sucked in a gasping breath as he leaned down and kissed her breasts.

He thrust inside of her, taking the reins of their lovemaking. The tempo was even and she could feel the energy building inside of her. She met his rhythm and they worked together until her body begged for release. She slowed, this moment needed to last—who knew when she would get a chance like this again?

With a twist of her hips, he tensed between her thighs. "Not yet," she whispered in his ear. "You must wait."

He growled and pressed deeper inside of her, as if to tell her how close he was. She lifted her chin to the stars, closed her eyes and let him move faster and faster inside of her. Her body tingled as her precipice neared.

He groaned deep, guttural, and animalistic as his warmth filled her. She opened her eyes and watched him while her body exploded in response to him. His body moved with her need as if he could read her mind.

Spent, she laid her head on his shoulder and let the warm water lap against her tired body.

They said nothing. Her legs stay wrapped around his body as he ran his fingers up and down her skin under the water. The haze of the ouzo had begun to lift, but was replaced by the lulling effect of the water and their romp.

He took his hand from the water and pushed a stray hair back behind her ear. "I've wanted to do that from the first moment I met you."

She had wanted this too, this freedom to make a choice unaffected by the constraints of her everyday life, outside of the contaminating opinions of her sisters, without the fear of the curse, and without worrying about Stavros.

Stavros? Why do I have to think of Stavros? I don't have to live consumed by the needs of the selfish, self-centered, pig-headed Stavros anymore. Her stomach flipped. *I'm free…*

Letting go of Beau, she threw her arms up into the air and she screamed. The happy sound filled the air.

Beau held her tightly, as if he supported her insanity.

Uncontrollable laughter took the place of her screaming. Freedom felt so good—so empowering.

Beau had a confused smile, but as she looked at him, he pulled her in tighter. Smiling, she kissed his lips. He was so warm, ambitious, sweet, caring, and for this moment—he was hers—only hers.

He pulled back from her lips, and smiled. "Are you okay?"

"I'm better than I've been in a long, long time." She dropped her feet from his waist and let the sand sift between her toes.

"Is this because of me? I hope…"

She brushed her lips against his cheek and stopped at his ear. "It's all because of you."

She made her way back to the beach, splashing Beau playfully as they moved. Beau stopped as the water reached his waist, glanced over at her and smiled. "Are you sure you're ready for all of this?" He motioned to his body beneath the waves.

"You're going to be shy now?" Ariadne giggled.

"No," he laughed. "I just don't want to blind you with my whiteness. Plus, it's not every day you get to see an American's pale cheeks."

She snickered. "I've seen more than my fair share of cheeks. I think I'll be able to recover from the shock."

He took her hand and led her from the water and to the pile of their clothes. She leaned back and looked at him in all the glory the water had masked. His arms and legs were covered in curly hair the same shade of brown as the hair on his head, while his chest was bare, which made the defined muscles of his core even more impressive.

He slid on his underwear and handed hers to her with a guilty smile. Suddenly embarrassed, she pushed her arm over her breasts.

"You look cold." Beau smiled. "I'll be right back."

While she brushed the sand from her clothes and pulled them over her chilled skin, he gathered driftwood from the beach. He stacked the pieces into a perfect pyramid, being careful to lean one piece against the other so that all could stand.

"There is always something that pulls me to fire," Ariadne said, as Beau sparked a match and lit a piece of the dried wood.

"Why?" He leaned into the tiny flame and blew gently, coaxing the timid flames to grow.

She thought back to the day she had given Theseus the ball of golden wire to lead him through the Labyrinth. Closing her eyes, she could still feel the all-encompassing darkness she had felt when she had followed him into the tunnel. The sounds of water as it dripped and splashed against the floor of the cave echoed in her mind. She had so badly wanted to start a fire in that place, to warm the chill that invaded her heart and create a sense of safety inside those walls and tunnels.

In all the years, she hadn't forgotten the sounds of the moans that circled up from the depths. It still amazed her that the lying, cheating, bastard Theseus had been brave enough to slay the Minotaur—but those had been the days when they had been in love.

It wasn't long after that fateful night that the curse of the nymph—and Zeus' minion, Athena—had lured him from her. She could still remember the way his black sails had billowed in the thin light of the moon, as he sailed off and left her alone on the beach. The pain of watching him go had left her with a wound that had never healed. When she had heard he had been killed, an immense sense of guilt had filled her. Could she have stopped him from leaving? What if she had been a better lover? Tried harder?

That was the first taste she had of the truth of Zeus' powerful curse.

"Aria?" Beau asked softly. "Are you okay?"

"Yes," She shook her head, trying to rid her mind of her thoughts. "I'm fine."

She stared into the orange, blue, and green flames of the salt-filled deadwood. Beau came over to her, sat down, and put his arm over her shoulders. She leaned against him, feeling the warmth of his skin through the thin fabric of her shirt.

Reaching down, he lifted her hand. He slowly traced lines up the dark edges of her tattoo. He pushed open her hand, exposing her palm and the head of the leopard snake. She fought the urge to pull away from his curious touch.

He ran his finger over the skin of her palm. "Did this hurt?"

"I received this when I was young. I don't really remember the pain."

"What does it mean?"

She pulled her hand away and tucked it under her legs. He didn't need to know about her. It would only open the door for danger—this could be nothing more than one night.

The flames flickered in his brown eyes as he stared at her. Touching his lips with her finger, she traced their outline, and ran her finger down his straight jaw. He lifted her fingers, pulled them to his lips, and kissed them one by one, as if he was marking his territory.

She moved on top of him, straddling him with her legs. His kiss was fierce, uncompromising, and almost angry.

"It's too bad you won't be able to go again." Ariadne gestured toward his manhood. She looked up with a wicked smile on her lips.

"You want to make a bet?"

He pulled up her skirt, exposing her thighs and ripped off her panties. He flipped her onto her back and drove himself inside her. He thrust deep as if to show her exactly how wrong she had been. Their lovemaking was wild and unchained, a throwback to the unchecked nights of her youth.

When they finished, they laid in the sand. Her head rested on his chest while she listened to the sounds of his body.

"Did you know those men at the bar?" he asked, breaking the sweet silence.

She should've known this was coming. Being a scientist meant he could never let things go. Of course he would want answers. "Not well…but this is a small island."

He ran his fingers through her hair. "The barkeeper didn't actually put rat poison in their bottle did she?"

The mouse has done worse things. "It's possible."

Beau lifted his head and looked down at her. "You can't be serious."

"There are a lot of things that happen on this island that outsiders wouldn't understand."

He stared at her. "You mean like you being the governor's girlfriend?"

She jerked out of his arms and sat up as her anger flared from his incendiary question. "What's not to understand about that?"

He sat up. "I just don't understand what he and you have in common. He seems like such a…an ass."

She smirked.

Beau looked down at the sand beneath his feet. "Did you have anything to do with his shooting?"

So even Beau thinks I'm to blame? The pain of his accusation was immediate. Did he really think she was the type of person that would try to kill her former partner?

"What if I said 'yes'?" she snarled.

Beau reached for her, but she moved away. "I'm sorry. I shouldn't have asked. Just the police kept asking me questions about you and Stavros and your…relationship."

"Well…I'm a curator, not a murderer."

"I'm sorry. All I was thinking was if you had something to do with the attempt, letting the barkeep poison those men wouldn't help your case."

"It won't kill them, just make them uncomfortable for a couple of days. And besides, you were just as angry with those men as I was. Don't sit there and act superior when you are the one who actually *paid* for their drinks."

"I didn't know what I was getting into." Anger dripped from his voice.

She glared at him. "What are you going to do now that your site is closed?"

He stared at her with a hurt expression on his face and guilt filled her, but was quickly replaced by irritation. He was the one who thought she was a killer.

He looked at his fingers, then back at her. "I told you, I'm going to fight. I'm going to get new grants and I'm going to get the police to reopen the site. The governor's shooting might not have been related to my work. I just need to make them realize how important my work is and get them to change their minds."

She stood up and grabbed her bag. "Well, good luck. When you get back to the States, don't worry about calling—you wouldn't want to get mixed up with a murderer…I'm sure it would be bad for your career."

Chapter Ten

Shaking the sand from his hair, Beau trudged up the stairs toward the apartment. It was getting late. Hopefully Kaden's night had been less eventful and Trina remained sane—unlike Ariadne.

He hadn't tried to upset her—though he could see where she was offended when he'd asked if she had anything to do with Stavros' shooting. He'd been out of line, but he had apologized. Wasn't it better that he asked her and been up front about what he had heard? Of course, he had thought she would say she had nothing to do with the shooting. But wasn't it better to ask? Who would've thought she would go ballistic about a simple question?

On the other hand, before they had fought, tonight had been the best night since…well, ever. Kaden's birth had been special, but a different type of special—plus, back then he'd been dealing with Lynda's infidelity. Her actions had tainted that special day, but from the moment that boy was born, Kaden was all his¾big eyes, chubby face, and all. There was never another question about the paternity of his son.

Why hadn't Ariadne had kids? Had she never met the right guy? Had the governor not wanted them? Had *she* not wanted them? She had been so good with Kaden at the museum. But was he part of the reason she had started a fight and run away? Was a man with a kid too much for her to handle?

He grabbed the keys from his pants pocket. Sliding the key into the lock, he pushed open the door. There on the bed, with a naked Trina perched on his lap, was Kaden.

Oh, Jesus Christ…

Trina must not have noticed the door, and kept moving.

Beau turned his back to the scene. "Trina? You need to get your clothes on. Kaden, I will meet you in the hall."

Trina emitted an embarrassed squeal as her feet pounded on the floor behind him.

Beau stepped out into the hall and slammed the door shut. He leaned against the wall and dropped his head. How was he going to handle this? Why had Lynda thrown him to the teenage wolves? This was advanced parenting, not have-the-kid-for-a-few-weeks parenting.

His son was a senior in high school. Kaden clearly knew about the birds and the bees. Could he really get mad at the kid? Yes, it wasn't great that it was happening, but when Beau had been in high school, it had been the goal to get where he just found Kaden.

Wouldn't he be a hypocrite for criticizing his son when, not a few hours before, Beau had been swimming naked with another Greek woman? Like father, like son, right?

He rubbed his hand roughly on his face. *I'm the father. I need to act like one.*

The door cracked open and Kaden walked out, his shirt wrinkled and his pants crooked. Kaden leaned against the wall next to him, and pushed his hands over his hair as he tried to smooth down the untamed mess. He looked sickly pale.

Beau didn't know how to start. A moment passed where neither said a word.

Finally, he forced himself to break the tense silence. "Kae, I think it's great you have a nice girlfriend."

Kaden snorted cynically.

"No, really. Trina is…great. But before you jump into such a *physical* relationship, I think you need to think about the possible consequences."

Kaden's cheeks reddened. "We used protection."

At least I won't have to have the contraception talk.

"I'm glad, but I wasn't just talking about getting her pregnant." Beau silently shook his head. Never in his life did he think he would be having this conversation. Nothing could've prepared him for the confusion and embarrassment. Poor Kae had to be feeling worse.

"Kaden, do you think Trina cares for you? Or is this just a fling?"

"Trina loves me and I love her."

Beau sucked in his breath. This was going to be harder than he thought.

"That's good…I mean that you wouldn't just jump into bed with a girl you don't really care about."

Kaden looked up, his face crunched into an ugly scowl. "What did you think? I was just using her to get laid?"

"No…that's not what I'm saying," Beau said softly. *This is a disaster.*

He didn't want to lose what little respect his son held for him by pitting his son against him. He needed to get him on the same page.

"Kaden, how long do you think you're going to stay here with me? You *do* know that my funding is running out, right?"

Kaden nodded.

"In two weeks, we'll have to leave and never come back." Beau's heart tightened in his chest as he said the words.

He was still angry, but the thought of never seeing Ariadne again—not as a friend, colleague, and never again as a lover—made his heart ache. Adding the fact that his site was closed and he may never get to finish what he had started, made the pain almost unbearable.

"If you love Trina, it's not a good idea to take things any farther. It'll only make it harder for both of you when we have to leave."

Kaden looked at the door as it cracked open. Trina walked out, her hair perfectly brushed.

"Dr. Morris, I need to apologize." Trina clicked the door shut. "It wasn't Kaden's fault. I'm the one to blame."

"Stop. You're not to blame."

I should've been paying more attention to my son.

Kaden reached over and took Trina's shaking hands.

"I just want the best for both of you. That's all." Beau said, unable to take his eyes off their entwined fingers.

"Thank you, Dr. Morris." Trina whispered.

"As it is, Trina, I think you should go."

Trina looked up at him as a tear slipped down her cheek. She nodded and dropped Kaden's hands.

"Don't go, Trina," Kaden begged. "He's just jealous because he doesn't have anyone."

Beau's stomach dropped. His first reaction was to rage. Who did Kaden think he was to talk to him like that? Kaden didn't know him, or about his personal life. His jaw clenched as he ground his teeth.

The hormones were behind his son's defiance. Rational thought was at a loss to the adolescent demons.

Beau stared at Kaden. The kid just didn't understand, life was hard and he was only trying to stop Kaden from getting hurt. "Trina. He'll see you again, but for right now you need to go."

Trina turned to Kaden. "Your dad's right. This doesn't mean that I won't see you again. Don't forget that I love you." Kaden seemed to calm with Trina's voice. "We'll respect your father's wishes. He only wants what's best."

Trina was way out of Kaden's league. She was so mature. Way too poised for eighteen.

Beau touched Trina's shoulder. "Thanks."

Trina turned to face him. "You're welcome. I'll stay away for a few days. Let things get back to normal for you."

She kept shocking him. It was easy to see why Kaden was so smitten with the beautiful young woman that stood before him.

"Yeah, that would be great." He and Kaden would need some time.

*

The morning had been occupied fielding questions from his students. Most were glad that they would have the last few weeks of their summer off so that they could travel around Europe. A few were upset that they wouldn't be able to finish the dig, but even they had been swayed to see the bright side of the predicament. His assistant looked almost relieved that he wouldn't have to deal with any more antics. Vickie had only nodded and smiled.

Beau hadn't mentioned the funding; the police filing an injunction was enough for them to handle. Instead, he reaffirmed that some of them would be invited to return the next summer.

The rest of the afternoon was filled with phone calls with the investigators, emails to colleagues, and what could be best described as silent ambivalence between Beau and Kaden. Kaden sulked on the bed and refused to talk to Beau, regardless of how hard Beau tried to elicit a response.

Beau leaned back from the computer and rubbed his eyes. Nothing was panning out for grants and he was getting nowhere in stopping the injunction. What he really wanted to do was hear someone laugh—to make someone happy, at least for a moment.

He looked over at Kaden. "You hungry?"

Kaden's gaze snapped to the window.

Weren't boys supposed to be easier to deal with?

"Kaden, you have to be hungry."

Kaden folded his arms over his chest.

Beau sighed, as he tried to be patient. "Get up and get your shoes on. We're bugging out."

Kaden emitted a wet cough as he slid his legs over the side of the bed and tied his shoes. At least he hadn't tuned him out completely. He would take what he could get with the kid.

They made their way around the town, until Beau found a café with a group of little wooden tables scattered out front. Kaden needed some fresh air and sunshine. He was looking paler than ever.

They made their way to a table and he pointed for Kaden to sit.

"Have you talked to your mother lately?" What he really wanted to ask was if he had told his mother what had transpired, but that seemed just a bit too pushy. Besides, if he had told his mother, Beau would have certainly gotten a call from her by now. Unless she thought it was funny.

Kaden shook his head.

"Bet she's missing you." Things were going downhill. Since when had he ever resorted to talking about Lynda to make conversation?

He needed to try another approach. "I think Trina's a nice girl. You picked well."

Kaden looked up from the table and frowned. "Yeah, she's great." Kaden bit his lower lip, as if he was holding back from saying more.

"I didn't mean to embarrass you last night, I hope you know that. I just want what's best for you."

Kaden picked up a napkin from the table and twisted it in his fingers. "I know," he said in almost a whisper.

Finally, progress.

A lanky waitress approached their table. Her brunette hair fell long over her shoulder and reminded him of Ariadne. Would Ariadne have a better way to handle this situation? He wished he could call her and get her advice, but he wasn't about to call her. She was the one who had acted crazy the other night. Then again, he hadn't helped anything.

It seemed like his life was in a downward spiral of chaos. What had he done to deserve all this shit? He paid his taxes, he didn't cheat, he didn't lie, yet he couldn't seem to get away from the bitch-slap of karma.

Now wasn't the time for self-pity. He needed to deal with everything. Kaden was more important than his self-pity. He needed to be there for his son.

The waitress smiled. "Can I get you something?"

Damn, even her voice was like Ariadne's. How was he going to make things right between them?

"I'll have a soda," Kaden said to the woman.

"Make that two." Beau picked up a menu and pointed at the first offering. "And an order of moussaka."

The woman smiled, took the menus, and fluttered away back into the white stucco building.

Beau tapped his finger on the metal mesh of the table as they waited. After a few minutes, he couldn't stand the silence between them any longer. "I want you to know, I'm really glad you came here to spend time with me."

Kaden still twisted the napkin between his fingers. "Well, Mom made me. It wasn't my choice."

Didn't Kaden understand that he was really trying? "I guessed that much, but I'm still glad you're here."

He could almost hear the nose-dive of a plane in his subconscious.

The waitress came back with two sweating glasses of soda, plates, a basket of bread, and a square dish of moussaka. "Here you boys go. Anything else for you?"

How about a way to get around Kaden's wall?

Beau forced a smile. "Nope. We're good. Thanks."

He noticed Kaden's glance follow the woman into the restaurant. He smiled. It was good sign to see his son doing something normal that wasn't moping.

"She's pretty, huh?" He waited for Kaden to respond. Nothing.

"Yeah, but she's not as pretty as Trina," Beau teased.

"Beau!" Kaden retorted. "That's gross."

"What?" Beau asked, trying to act innocent. "Just saying that Trina's *hot.*"

"Oh my God. You didn't really just say that did you?"

"Hmm?" Beau scooped out some of the lasagna-looking dish

and dropped it on Kaden's plate, then his own, as he tried not to laugh. He'd found the sweet spot.

Kaden picked at his food. "Don't talk about her like that…"

Beau ate a bite of the delicious melted cheese and vegetables and took a moment to savor the rich flavors, and let his son linger in thought.

Beau swallowed and took a sip of his soda. "I'm just saying at least my kid has good taste. Good thing too, your mother said you were having a hard time with the girls at school. I thought I was going to have to set you up with one of the old nuns."

Kaden smiled, as he must have realized Beau was teasing. "Yeah, Trina's hot. But that Ariadne—man!" Kaden's eyes bore into him. "When are you going to go after that? She seemed like she needs a good—"

"A good what?" Beau asked, as his eyebrows rose.

Kaden laughed. "I was going to say 'guy.' What did you think I was going to say, Beau?"

Chapter Eleven

Ariadne looked up at the night sky. The clouds rolled across the heavens and blotted out the light of the moon, darkening the sisterhood's festivities. It was strange to think that only a night ago, she and Beau had been below in the bay making love as if tomorrow would never come. Why had she allowed her need for his touch override her judgment of what should and shouldn't be done?

Near the edge of the circular fire pit, where the tiny tips of orange flames reached upwards, Tammy stood with a bag at her feet. Arrayed around Tammy were Ariadne's serpent-shifting sisters. At the head of the circle sat a half-log altar, and behind it a group of sisters sat while they beat large drums in an old melody. Tammy threw her arms into the air and began to chant in unison with the beat.

Kat stepped next to Ariadne's left and slid her cold hand into Ariadne's. Kat looked at her and smiled as she dug her nails painfully into her skin. Looking the woman in the eye, Ariadne smiled though the pain shot through her.

"I assume you will be following directions tonight." Kat glared at her. "I hope I don't need to reinforce to you the importance of this ceremony. I've heard about how close you have become with that Dr. Morris. Don't you dare, for a second, assume that I'm not aware of how you're behaving. You need to end the relationship now. I won't allow it."

Kat's power trip was getting on her nerves. When would it end? When would Kat treat her with respect?

Though she was mad at Beau for the way he had treated her, something in her had changed last night. There would be no going back to being a meek little lamb. She needed to live her life, and she couldn't do that if she continued to be pushed down by Kat. However, tonight was not the time to let hatred take center stage. Every woman of the circle was a sister, even Kat, and they had come together to honor their goddess.

Instead of answering, she simply turned her back on the woman and walked to the far side of the circle and took the hands of her other sisters.

Kat walked next to Tammy and pulled a snake out of the bag that sat at Tammy's feet. The snake wrapped its thick, brown body around her naked thigh and Kat began to sing a hymn to Epione. The drums beat strong and with each thunderous quake the snake slithered farther up the woman, winding over her arms and then up around her neck. The woman didn't flinch; instead, her red lips pulled into a crazed smile while her eyes reflected the lingering flames of the ebbing fire.

The crowd around Tammy filled the circle with a garble of prayers. Ariadne's heart mimicked the beat of their wavering tones and her stomach clenched with the tension that grew with each thunderous beat of the drum.

Ariadne had been a part of the ceremony every year for almost three thousand years, but it still felt as sacred and monumental as the first time she had celebrated the human death of her goddess, the day Zeus chose to encase their island in the molten rock of Thera. He had killed thousands of Minoans, and ended an egalitarian society that would never again find a foothold in human culture.

Zeus had always hated the fact that women had been the central focus of the culture. Women lawmakers, business owners, and empresses—and the dismissal of his sexual advance toward Epione had only been a reason for him to eradicate the peaceful society.

Ariadne would never forget the day the ash had rained down from the sky. The ground had rumbled beneath her feet and day turned into night. She and her sisters had run to take shelter, but many were buried by the falling ash, only to be found days or weeks later.

Epione had fallen to Zeus, but not before she had entrusted the care of her staff to Kat, who had followed her wishes and brought the twisted crystal staff to the Labyrinth—where it had stayed. And where it needed to remain, protected.

The wind blew, billowing the thin fabric of her skirt and teasing the flames.

She closed her eyes and exhaled a calming breath. Now was the time. "Goddess, be with me."

She stepped out from her place in the circle and walked to the altar. Reverently, she picked up the ceramic statue of Epione, their goddess, their mother, and the first of their kind. Her powers had been magnificent, the ability to heal, perform magic, sing and dance. Unfortunately, as she bore more nymphs, her powers were passed on, but lessened with each successive generation. Now most nymphs had one special power and one shift, and typically that was all. Epione was an amazing goddess. More than a goddess— she was everything—an amazing woman, friend, and mother.

With a bow, she lifted the idol and placed it lovingly in her arms. She needed to concentrate on the task at hand and serve her goddess well.

The chant continued, but she found silence in her soul as she prepared for what she must do. Turning, she walked to the edge of the wide fire pit. Her foot struck the hot coals, but there was no pain. The warmth of the ground was like the touch of a mother's warm hands on her sensitive feet.

Taking a step, she looked down at the ancient sculpture of the wide-armed goddess perched inside the security of her arms. The snakes wrapped around the goddess' arms and wound in a sacral knot between her bare breasts. The sculpture grew hotter in her arm as it absorbed the heat from the flames.

"You are safe, my mother," she prayed. "The flames shall not touch my mother, my goddess. May they only warm the hearts of those who remember your sacrifice. May they honor your memory, and move past the transgression inflicted upon us. I vow to protect you, our way of life, and all that we hold sacred." She closed her eyes and a sense of peace passed over her.

Her feet struck the cool grass as she left the heat of the flames. She walked to the half-log altar that was covered in the fruits, grapes, oils, and honeys that she and her sisters had brought in tribute to their goddess. With a bow, she gently placed the sculpture at the center of the altar. "Please help me to move forward with my life and escape the ghosts of my past." She dropped her head in a low bow. "Blessed be, my mother."

She kissed the smooth edge of Epione's ceramic skirt. A tear slid down her cheek as she remembered her mother. It would have been so different if Zeus had only chosen another, more willing woman.

Her hands shook as she lifted her lips from the hem of her goddess' skirt. Epione had sacrificed for what she knew was right. She had given her life to not be violated by a man—no, a God. Now it was time for her and her sisters to honor her sacrifice with a sacrifice of their own.

The white yearling goat stood picketed at the far end of the circle. It called out into the night, as if the beast knew what was to come.

Stepping back, Ariadne picked up her long hair and flipped it under her shirt. Peeling the edges of the cotton from her stomach, she pulled the shirt off and dropped it to the ground. Her sisters followed her lead and each began shedding the skin of their society. Her white skirt fell to the green grass and she stepped her blackened, ash-covered feet from the circle the fabric formed.

Everyone went silent as they stripped from their clothes. Trina, the youngest sister, stepped to the stake and took the goat's leash. The goat bleated, as she led the untouched beast to Kat.

Kat lifted the head of the snake from her wrist. Pinching its diamond-shaped head, she pressed it to the neck of the goat. Again and again she pressed the snake's fangs into the flesh of the sacrifice. The goat began to shift and lean. Kat laughed as she pressed the fangs of the snake into the goat again.

The goat bleated and fell to the ground. Its side rose with shallow breaths. Kat pulled the snake from her body and kissed the head of the snake. With quiet veneration, she bent down and rested the serpent on the body of the goat.

Tears welled in Ariadne's eyes, this was a part of the sacrifice, but it always made her sad to watch an innocent animal give its life. She blinked back her tears. She had a low enough rank without having her sisters assume that the modern world had weakened her devotion to their goddess.

"My sisters," Kat exclaimed, extending her arms into the sky, in the stance of the snake goddess figurine. "We dance!"

The naked women pulled together into a circle around the flickering ashes. Each woman took the next hand. Ariadne took Trina's hand and smiled. The young nymph had only experienced this ceremony for a few hundred years, and her excitement was still fresh on her face. Kat pushed her way between them, and grabbed Ariadne's hand. Ariadne ignored the way Kat's fingernails scraped her skin.

Kat led them into the Greek song. *"Epione, my humble goddess. Ever present to bring health to the sick. Epione, battle-maiden of death, we salute you. Bring us this day a new year filled with life. May the curse of Zeus be lifted and your bravery be commended."*

Letting go of Kat's hand, their song ceased and she spun out into the night. She rubbed the blood back into her fingertips as she wove her naked body in a wide arc around the other women. Kat looked over her bare shoulder and back toward her. Catching her eye, Kat sneered and turned back toward the flames, her bubble-shaped behind looked even larger in the poor light.

Ariadne smiled as she let the darkness take her naked form.

The women began to move slowly in a rhythmic dance around the flames. They hummed an ancient song. While she watched, she moved back into the row of heavily scented olive trees. She needed a moment away from the prying eyes of her sisters to rest.

A warm hand grasped her wrist and she tried to scream, but another clapped over her mouth. She tried to pull away from the hands, but as she struggled, the man's hands only grew stronger. He pulled her toward him. She could feel the heat of his body against her naked back and his breath tickled the nape of her neck.

"Don't speak," a man whispered. "I'm not going to hurt you."

Her teeth grazed his flesh as she tried to bite the inside of his hand.

"Hey, no," he warned.

She wanted to shift, but to do so was dangerous. The man smelled of human.

"Let go," she said, her words garbled by the sweat of his palm.

"If I let you go, you must promise not to alert your friends."

If she agreed, there was no guarantee that the stranger wouldn't try to kill her, not that he could. His hands were full now, but if he let go, he would be free to do as he pleased. She was naked and weaponless—expect for her serpent form. If she shifted, she would have to strike, and with her strike came death.

Should she kill him?

"Who the hell do you think you are?" she demanded through his slightly opened fingers.

"I am…" he hesitated, "not the one standing here naked."

The pressure of the man's hands lightened and she spun around in his encircling arms. Beau stood looking at her with a look of shock upon his face.

She looked down at her brown erect nipples.

Damn it.

She shoved her arms over her breasts. He wouldn't get any more free shows.

"Do you make a habit of being a voyeur?"

He smiled, his dark eyes picked up the orange of the lingering flames behind her. His eyes were the color of the ocean at night, deep, clear, mysterious and alluring. He blinked and she could see the reflection of Kat in his eyes.

"So you do like watching naked women?" She pressed her hands against his chest. The muscles under her fingers tensed and quivered with her touch. She thought back to the way his hands had felt the night before.

He looked past her at the group of woman around the fire. "What the hell?" he muttered as he squinted in the direction of the fallen animal. "Is that a goat?"

She was still angry with his accusations, but seeing him here made her forget for a moment the hurt feelings. "What are you doing here, Beau?"

"What the hell are you involved in?" Beau's gaze bore into her.

"You shouldn't be here." She took his hand and, looking back over her shoulder to make sure no one had seen her go, pulled him away from the ceremony and down the hill.

The hillside was steep and rocks tumbled and fell to the beach below. The rocks tore at her feet; she should've gone back and gotten some clothing and shoes, but she couldn't risk Beau being seen. He was in enough danger just seeing what he had, without being noticed by a group of women who wholeheartedly believed him to be their enemy.

She should've never shown him the bay. Once again, he had amplified the danger for her kind. If he told anyone about what he had seen… Some people would think she and her sisters were crazy, but undoubtedly there would be a few that would connect the dots—then their real enemies would descend upon them.

The snake goddess sisterhood was a powerful group. For witches and sorcerers, just a handful of skins would be priceless and, if destroyed, prove deadly to the nymph to which they belonged.

And if anyone found their way to the Labyrinth, what would happen to Epione and the staff—only the goddess knew—but the sisterhood couldn't afford another battle.

She should've never let him be anything besides an enemy. At least he would be leaving Crete soon, and with him the danger he created for the nymphs.

Beau fumbled down the hillside behind her, cussing and sliding as the crumbling rocks gave way beneath his feet. It was doubtful with all the commotion that the nymphs would hear the stones falling over their rhythm chants and the pounding drums.

Picking her way through the rocks, she made her way to the water's edge, Beau at her side. The waves poured over her feet washing away the droplets of blood left by the sharp edges of the stones. She wrapped her arms around herself and closed her eyes, letting the salty brine sting her open wounds.

"Are you okay?" Beau pointed at her feet.

"I'm fine," she huffed, as she tried to think of a way to lie to cover the ceremony he had just witnessed.

"Here." He pulled his fleece jacket from his arms and draped it over her. "You look cold."

"Thanks." She pulled the jacket tight over her body, covering her exposed flesh all the way to her knees. "Beau, what were you doing up there?"

"Beau? Hey, Beau?" Kaden's voice sounded from farther down the beach.

Beau grabbed her hand and squeezed, as if telling her to remain quiet. "We're right here."

She should've pulled her hand from his, but she felt no urge. Instead, she let his warmth seep through her, just as she had before. It felt good to be touched by him, even if it was only for a moment, even if it was something that could never last.

For a moment, she imagined what it would be like to be married to a man like Beau, traveling the world with his son, investigating the mysteries of the forgotten past. If he knew about her, they could work together. She could teach him about the secrets that humanity had forgotten.

The future she envisioned could never be. Humans would never accept that there were beings different from themselves—especially not nymphs—shape-shifting seductresses. Instead, they would be used as another reason for humans to judge, hate, and ostracize. The potential of humans knowing that magic was real, that there were immortals, and the potential to live forever, would only mean ideological wars.

"Who's we?" Kaden yelled, pulling her from her confusion.

"Ariadne was the partier." Beau forced a laugh, but even in the thin moonlight, she could see that his eyes were filled with unanswered questions.

"Did Kaden see, too?" Ariadne whispered harshly, looking away from his probing gaze.

"No, he was swimming. He hasn't been feeling well, so I left him down here. But you are going to need to answer for what was going on up there."

She looked down at the coat, luckily it was long enough to cover everything that needed to be covered. The sounds of the drums echoed down into the bay, where only a few nights before they had been making love. His hand loosened around hers and his thumb rubbed against her skin, just as it had done so when she had been well-plied with ouzo. She looked down at his hand as it pressed against hers. Her pale hand looked out of place in his rough, tanned hand.

At least she wouldn't have to worry about lying to the boy—only his father.

"When we're alone…," she mumbled.

"Fine, but I hope you'll be naked again." He flashed a dangerous smile. "I can only hold back so much, and watching you dance around naked was almost more than I could handle."

He pulled her hand to him and his lips pressed against her skin. She could feel the desire that pulsed within him, just as she had in the surf. She felt a tingle between her thighs. It would feel so good to have him again.

Kaden splashed toward her, huffing as if he had walked a mile instead of the few hundred yards it had been. "Why didn't you invite us to the party?" Kaden asked, with a winded laugh.

She smiled. "Sorry, Kae…I promise it wouldn't have been your thing."

Kaden coughed. "Sorry, I'm not—" His cough cut off his words. He tried to suck in a breath, but she watched him struggle as another rattling cough took over his body.

"Kaden?" Beau cried.

The boy looked at his father as tears flowed down his face. The young man hacked, unable to control the coughing as it took over his body. He dropped to his knees in the sand.

Ariadne and Beau kneeled beside him. Beau put his hand on his son's back. "Kaden?" Beau's voice was strangled.

Kaden coughed again, his body rattled and shook and blood splattered on the sand. Kaden looked up and blood dripped from his mouth, down his chin.

Beau glanced at Ariadne. He reached in his back pocket, pulled out his cell phone and thrust it at her. "Call an ambulance."

Chapter Twelve

The taxi ride home from the hospital seemed like hours instead of only the thirty minutes it had taken. Ariadne sprinted in and grabbed the first dress she saw and slipped it over her shoulders. She pulled out her car keys and ran out the door. Her hands shook on the drive back to the hospital as she silently prayed that Kaden would be okay.

Beau met her outside the revolving hospital doors. "Thanks for coming back, I know this has to be awkward for you, but I appreciate you being here. It's nice to not have to go at this alone."

Her cheeks flushed. "You asked me to be here." She shoved her keys in her purse as she hurried inside, Beau close behind her. "Is he doing any better?"

"The doctors have done some x-rays and they took blood right after you left. We should be hearing something soon," Beau said, twisting the watch on his wrist.

"It'll be okay, Beau." She put her hand to his face and brushed a loose strand of hair behind his ear.

When they walked into the private room, Kaden tried to sit up, but fell back into the white sheets. "Hi, guys." A cough rattled from his lips.

"Hey, Kae." Ariadne stepped beside him and put her hand on his shoulder. "You're looking better," she lied.

"Do you need anything? Soda? Water? Pillow?" Beau stepped up to the bed, next to Kaden's feet.

"No," Kaden wheezed. "I'm good."

The blood pressure cuff ballooned on Kaden's arm and released with a wheeze. "You okay?" Beau asked, moving to his son's side.

"I'm fine, Dad. Promise. It's just taking my blood pressure." Kaden pushed the button on the bed rail to sit up. While the bed

whirred upward, he motioned for Beau to sit down in the mauve vinyl chair by the window.

A knock interrupted the pair and Ariadne stepped to the door. Before she could reach the door, a stern-faced doctor in a white lab coat and a blue face mask walked into the room. He was carrying a clipboard and he clicked his pen nervously.

Beau stood up and let the doctor step to the side of Kaden's hospital bed.

"Hello, I'm Dr. Dukakis." The thin, gray-haired man stopped clicking and offered his blue-gloved hand to Kaden.

Ariadne was sure he meant for the handshake to be comforting, but the way the doctor slightly withdrew when Kaden reached for his hand made her fear the worst.

The doctor turned to Beau and nodded. "What's going on?" Beau blurted out.

The doctor's gaze settled on Kaden. "We've gotten the results from your tests."

"And?" Beau insisted.

The doctor looked back at Beau. His face was stoic, but his eyes were filled with identifiable pity.

"Are you the boy's father?" the doctor asked.

"Yes. What'd you find out?"

"Well, sir, after reviewing the lab and x-ray results, it looks like your son has contracted what we call active tuberculosis."

Beau sank to the chair behind him. "Tuberculosis?" he uttered, his gaze flickered to his son. "Okay," he said louder, more assuredly. "Tuberculosis is treatable. When are you planning on beginning the antibiotics?"

"That's what I want to talk to you about." The doctor's voice was grim. He pulled at the collar of his jacket. "I can't be sure until we run further tests. The lab results were inconclusive, but it currently looks as though his tuberculosis is from the resistant strain."

"Resistant strain?" Ariadne spoke up. "You mean you can't treat him?"

The doctor looked at her. "Like I said, we'll have to run a few more tests. In the meantime, we will start treatment with a combination of Isoniazid, Rifampin, and Ethambutol. If it is the treatable strain, that should begin to kill the bacterium before there is more significant damage."

"What do you mean *more significant damage*?" Beau rumbled.

The doctor stepped back toward the open door. "If this strain is treatable, we won't need to worry. If not, well, in most cases the bacteria will begin to affect the heart, kidneys, and liver. There is also a slight possibility the bacteria could move into the brain and cause meningitis. We need to get on this and treat him prophylactically for the treatable strain."

"Yes. Go. Get it started," Beau ordered.

There was a crazed look in his eyes, a look filled with fear, anger, confusion, and determination. In another moment, it would have been sexy, but in the moment, it only made fear rise within her.

The doctor wrote something on his clipboard. "There are some possible side effects from the drugs, but if this is the treatable strain, he can stay at home while he undergoes treatment."

Beau stood up. "I understand. But just do what you need to do. Go. Get the drugs my son needs."

"Just so you know—best case, it will probably take at least eight weeks for him to be totally cleared." The doctor scanned the room, but no one spoke. They all just sat in stunned silence. There was no way Beau would be leaving the island with his son in the hospital.

The doctor pushed his pen into his pocket. "Before we can start, you both need to leave the room as soon as possible. Tuberculosis is contagious, especially if he is coughing. We are going to move him to a negative air pressure room and get him isolated."

Ariadne moved toward Kaden. His eyes were wide with fear.

"I'm not going anywhere," Beau challenged. "This is my son. I'm not leaving his side."

"I strongly recommend that you do. You're doing your son no favors by staying here and possibly contracting the disease."

The doctor reached into his pocket and handed Beau a business card. Beau grabbed it from his hands and shoved it into his back pocket.

The doctor pushed the clipboard under his arm and stepped to the door. "If you have any questions, you are welcome to call me. As soon as I get the culture results back from the lab, we'll know more. I'll make sure to get in contact with you."

"You do that." Beau stepped back, but his face was filled with anguish.

The door clicked shut behind the doctor.

The air of the hospital room was thick with concern. What were they going to do? How could she make this better? All of a sudden, Ariadne felt horribly out of place. This was a private family moment.

Beau stepped close to Kaden and she dropped the young man's hand. "Do you want me to go?" She pointed at the door.

"No," Beau said. "I need you."

Kaden looked at her and nodded weakly.

"What should I do?" Kaden's voice trembled with fear.

"It's going to be fine, Kae," Beau said, his voice resolute. "This is going to be treatable. Until we know for sure, we are going to take one day at a time. Don't worry. Everything will be fine."

"Beau…" Kaden looked at his father. "I mean, Dad…I love you."

Beau smiled, but as he looked away from Kaden, there were tears in his eyes. She had never heard Kaden call Beau "Dad" before, and from the look on Beau's face, the word was more than just a name.

"I love you, too, Kae." Beau patted Kaden's arm lovingly.

She swallowed back the emotions that threatened to spill over, but she couldn't stop the tears that welled in her eyes.

He dabbed his eyes as he turned to her. "I need to call his mother and let her know what they've found. Then I'll call Trina and tell her she needs to get tested for tuberculosis."

"No…I mean I can call Trina later. She might take the news best from me."

Beau stared at her for a long moment. "That's fine. Tell her I'm sorry. Okay?"

She nodded.

"Do you mind staying here?"

"No, go ahead." Of course Beau needed a moment alone, to collect himself. He needed to stay strong for his son.

Beau ran his hand lovingly over Kaden's hair and smiled. "I'll be back in a sec, cool?"

Kaden rolled his eyes. "I'm not dying, Dad."

Beau nodded and made his way to the door. "I know, kiddo. But I only got one of you, I'm allowed to worry."

The door clicked shut behind him.

Kaden's eyes were half closed, but he kept forcing them open.

Ariadne tried to smile. "Why don't you rest?"

Kaden nodded. Ariadne sat down in the vinyl chair next to the bed, slid her hand under his, and squeezed. He smiled and his head fell back to the pillow. In less than a minute, he was asleep.

While she watched Kaden's shallow breaths, her mind wandered to Beau. She could understand that he needed to talk to Kaden's mother. From the way Beau had spoken the words, there was no warmth, but she found little comfort in his inflection. Was there still some relationship between Beau and the woman? And why was she so taken aback by with the thought of Beau talking to another woman?

*

The phone rang on the other end of the line as he walked out the revolving glass doors of the hospital. A part of Beau wished that Lynda would ignore the call, that he could just tell her what she needed to know without actually having to speak to his ex-wife.

When she picked up, his stomach fell. He had only been in custody of their son for a few weeks and now he was forced to call her with unthinkable news. She was going to blame this on him.

"Hello?" Lynda questioned.

"Hi, Lynda. How's the honeymoon?" Beau asked, trying to sound civil.

"Great. We went to the Puerta del Sol last night. And tomorrow we're going to travel to Seville, then we're going on a cruise. It's going to be hot, but this is just such a once-in-a-lifetime trip," she said, sounding excited. She paused for a second, as if she remembered who she was talking to. "Why are you calling?"

"It's Kaden."

"Is he causing trouble again?" she snapped. "This is getting so goddamned old. You need to take care of it—"

"That's not it," he said, interrupting her rant.

"Then why would you call?"

"Lynda, I just admitted him into the hospital here in Heraklion."

"What?"

"He collapsed on the beach. The ambulance brought him here."

"Why didn't you call me before?" she chastised him.

"We only just talked to the doctor. I didn't want to interrupt you until I knew something."

The phone was silent.

"So what did the doctors say?" Lynda asked.

"They believe he has tuberculosis. They are about to start him on antibiotics, and they are going to move him into isolation."

Lynda tsked, as if she was thinking. "So it's treatable?"

"Hopefully, but I think it'd be nice if you could come back and at least see him. I think he's having a hard time with this."

"The antibiotics will clear the infection, won't they?" She sounded distant.

Lynda won't flake out on her sick child, will she?

"As long as the infection isn't the drug resistant kind…but I think you should be here," he urged, his voice filled with anger.

"We already bought our train passes and paid for our rooms. That's a lot of money we'd be losing."

"It's just money, Lynda. Don't you think your son is more important than your goddamned vacation?" He already knew how this was going to play out, but he went through the motions as he had with so many fights before.

"You said he's treatable, right?"

"I said 'hopefully.' They aren't sure, but he's going to be here for at least a few weeks before he isn't contagious."

"Well, see, there's really no point to me coming back if I can't even be around him. Just tell him I love him. Won't you?"

"I'm not your carrier pigeon. If you want to say something to your son, you should come here and tell him yourself."

Lynda sighed. "You are such a drama king."

"Our son is sick, and just because I think you should be here, I'm being dramatic?"

How had he ever fallen for a woman who was so devoid of normal human emotion?

"Maybe I'll come in a week," she offered begrudgingly. "We should be back from our cruise by then, we'd have to cancel the trip to Italy, but maybe if we rearranged a few things…"

He held back from yelling at her that she needed to get her ass there. Screaming at each other would accomplish nothing, it never had. Hopefully, with a little time, she would understand how important it was for her to be at her son's bedside. But she was going to have to come to the decision herself. He had done what he could.

He tried to sound satisfied. "Great. See you soon."

"Sure," she said, but she sounded uncertain. "Call me if anything changes. I should have service on the ship."

He slammed the phone shut. He slumped down on a bench and put his head in his hands. Poor Kaden, he deserved better than this.

*

Ariadne pulled a piece of lint from the dress she had grabbed from her closet. The dress reeked of the hospital antiseptic, but as strong as it was, it couldn't mask the distant odor of death and sadness. She couldn't wait to get the damned thing off.

Kaden shifted in the bed and opened his eyes. "Hey."

"You awake? Your dad's still gone."

Kaden shrugged and stared out the window.

Ariadne didn't know what to say. It had to be so hard for Kaden. No one this young should have to go through anything like this, but pity would help nothing. It was strange to think that not that long ago, she had felt so alone—part of nothing but the double-edged sisterhood. Holding Kaden's hand, she could feel the bond strengthen between them, almost like love.

"Tell me about the party. You know, the one on the top of the hill?" Kaden asked, breaking the awkward silence.

For a moment she considered telling him the truth, but telling him she had been dancing naked with the Sisterhood of Epione didn't want to roll off her tongue. She smiled at the thought of the questions that would follow. The young man would be open-minded enough to believe what she would tell him about nymphs and witches, elves and bulls, but would it help him? No.

Then it struck her. There was something that she could do to help Kaden. She thought about the crystal staff of Epione. If she found it, they could heal whatever ailed him. But it was impossible on so many levels.

Modern medicine was making progress every day. They would cure him. He and Beau would go back to America and then this confusing mess of emotions would come to an end.

"Aria?" Kaden pressed.

"Oh, sorry," she said, with a weak smile. "I was just thinking."

"About?" He tried to hold back a cough.

"You okay?"

He nodded.

She forced a bigger smile. "I was just thinking about how nice it has been to meet you and your dad."

Kaden looked at the door. "Yeah, my dad has really...come alive since he met you. Before it was all *the dig* and *funding*. Since you came into our lives, he...smiles."

He smiles? He seemed like such a happy man, at least most of the time. It was strange to think that he wasn't always the person she saw.

"But then again," Kaden continued. "I don't know him very well."

"What do you mean?" she inquired.

"Didn't he tell you?" He looked surprised.

She shook her head.

"The last time I saw him before Crete was ten years ago. He left me standing alone at the edge of our yard," Kaden paused. "The last thing he said was 'One day you'll understand love, kiddo.' But from what I can see, Beau doesn't understand it any better than I do."

She was taken aback with his candor and for a moment she just sat and thought about what to say. "Have you ever been in love?"

He looked down at their joined hands. "Up until now I thought I had, but Trina made me rethink everything I thought I knew. With Trina, it's like my heart is going to beat out of my chest every time she gets close to me. I even had to buy extra-strength deodorant." Their laughter filled the air.

"That's great, Kaden," she said, still laughing. "You know it's a good thing when you try not to smell."

Kaden's eyes sparkled with life and looked out of place against the pallor of his skin. "Trina's special. I really love her."

As his words sank in, Ariadne's heart fell. *It all makes sense why he's sick…he's in love with a nymph. The curse…*

She jumped to her feet and stumbled on the chair leg as she burst from the room. The door closed behind her, and without looking where she was going, she bumped into a man.

"I was wondering when you would come back to see me again," Stavros boomed.

She struggled to find her bearings as she stared at the man in the hospital gown with a gauze bandage wrapped around his neck. "Stavros?"

He looked at her with a squint. "You okay? You look tired."

No, she wasn't *okay*, but Stavros couldn't help. No one could help. If she had only told Trina to stop seeing Kaden, this wouldn't have happened. But wait…if Stavros would've just closed the site after she had found him in the office with Bunny, none of this would have happened. And an innocent teenager wouldn't be at risk.

"Goddamn you, Stavros." She pushed past him and began to run—anything to get away from the mess she had helped to create.

"Ariadne?" He called out after her, but she couldn't be stopped.

The revolving door of the hospital forced her to slow, and the second the warm morning air touched her skin, her guard fell. Tears flowed down her cheeks and she gasped for air, choking on her emotions. How had she let herself get mixed up with Beau and his son? Why had she allowed herself to feel? If only she was stronger.

Her vision was blurred with tears, but she kept moving down the sidewalk in the direction of her car.

"Ariadne?" Beau ran up beside her.

She looked at him through teary eyes, but before she could say anything, he pulled her into his arms. She pressed her face into the smooth cotton of his jacket and let her tears fall. His hands ran up and down her back. "It's okay. It's okay," he whispered repeatedly.

After a few minutes, his constant reassurance took effect and her tears stopped. She must look like a mess; she could just imagine her mascara running down her face and how red her eyes must be. Subtly, she tried to dab at her nose before she looked up.

"What's going on, sweetheart?" Beau asked his voice smooth and calm. "Is Kaden okay?"

"He's fine…" She realized how she must look to him, hysterical and crying. "I'm sorry. I hope I didn't scare you. I just realized…" she stopped herself.

He can't know the truth—that one of my sisters is responsible for inadvertently trying to kill his son.

"We can't do this, Beau," she stammered, motioning to the two of them.

"What?" he asked, confusion flashed across his face. "What are you saying?"

"You can't be with me. I can't be with you. This won't work." She pulled out of his arms and stepped back. "I planted the baby's remains in your site. I had to shut it down."

"What?" Beau growled. "You're lying. You wouldn't."

She looked down at asphalt.

He grabbed her by the arms, but she couldn't look up and see the hurt that would be in his eyes.

She was quiet for a moment, as she remembered that terrible night. "I left behind a pile of clothes, with a blue latex glove in the back pocket of my pants."

He dropped his hands as his breath left him. "You fucked with my site? You, a woman who can understand how important this is, disturbed a site that my career depends on?"

He took a step away as if she repulsed him. "Did you have

something to do with the shooting as well? Or am I to believe that was just an isolated incident?"

The tears were a steady stream. "No. I wouldn't—"

"Stop," he interrupted. "I don't believe anything you have to tell me."

"You're right," she said in a choked voice. "You deserve better than me."

"You know what?" He stepped back and glared at her. "I think you're right."

Chapter Thirteen

Walking into the office of the museum, Ariadne dropped her purse on her desk where a pile of newspapers sat neatly stacked at its center. The secretary must not have known she had been avoiding the news.

Ariadne thumbed through the week's papers, anything to take her mind off Beau and the mess she had left in her wake. Why had she let things go so far? Everything bad that was happening was her fault. She had spent the night tossing and turning. Sleep had never come and the only thing she decided with any certainty was that she, and her sisterhood, were evil.

The press was having a field day with the mystery still revolving around the governor's shooting. The headlines rapidly declined as the days went on. On the day of the shooting the headline read: "Governor Shot," the next day, "Questions Remain as to Shooter's Identity," to "American Archeologist Being Questioned for Role in Governor's Shooting," to the last and worst which read, "Archeology Site in Gournai Shut Down Indefinitely as Investigations Dig Deeper."

She read the first paragraph: "Beloved Governor Kakos is staying quiet about the events of Friday's shooting. Investigators believe foul play is involved. Captain Christos of the Hellenic Police Force has refused to comment, but witnesses of the shooting were heard saying that there had been a disagreement earlier that day between the archeologist, Beau Morris, and Governor Kakos regarding proposed funding of the site."

She skipped the gossip and read further down. "Governor Kakos' former girlfriend, Ariadne Papadakis, Heraklion Museum curator, has been spotted cavorting with Mr. Morris on numerous occasions. Which raises questions about the motives for the shooting…"

Raises questions about the motives? What did she have to do with the shooting? And just because she had been seen talking to Beau, how did that make the headlines? The reporters were pulling at scraps. They must not have any real answers for the shooting and were now resorting to making up the truth.

Did they really think that Beau had something to do with the governor's shooting? Beau was a lot of things, but he wasn't a man who would go around murdering other men. Beau was too kind, too caring. She would never forget the way he had rushed to his son's side, never wavered in his commitment to getting him healthy. He was such a good man—far too good of a man for her. She had ruined whatever could have been between them the moment she had planted the baby's body in his site.

She tried to push the thoughts of Beau from her mind. She needed to get past him. They couldn't be together. He was everything she couldn't have.

Her phone rang. She sat down at her desk and pulled it from her slumped purse. "Hello?"

"Ms. Papadakis?" an authoritative voice questioned.

"Yes?"

"This is Captain Christos, of the Hellenic Police Force."

Her cheeks flushed. "Hello, Christos. What can I do for you?" she asked, trying to sound above suspicion.

He coughed lightly. "I have a few questions about the events of the other day as well as some regarding your developing relationship with Mr. Morris."

Her heart sank. The captain wasn't the only one with questions about her future with Beau.

"Sure, but I already told you everything I know."

"Great, then it shouldn't take long. Do you think you could meet me for lunch? There's a great café close to the museum, you've probably been there but—"

If she didn't go, he would have more questions, and more

suspicion. She huffed. She could only deflect for so long, but she wasn't ready to face the interrogation. "I'm sorry, I have plans."

"I see." He sounded dangerous.

"Maybe tomorrow?" She tried to recover.

"I'm sure I will see you before that. Good bye," the captain said, his tone clipped. The line clicked as he hung up.

The journalists may have thought Beau was behind the shooting, but apparently, the captain was still sniffing around her.

Well, he would find nothing.

She clicked the phone shut and dropped her arms on top of the pile of papers. How had she gotten herself mixed up in all of this? Last week she had been a quiet, somewhat respected museum curator with a powerful boyfriend, and this week she was a confused, suspicious, enemy-embracing…rebel.

She dropped her forehead down onto the papers and closed her eyes. At least Beau's site was closed, her sisters would be grateful. He wasn't going to be a problem to them as long as he wasn't digging.

Her office door slammed open. Startled, she sat up as Kat pranced into the room, her high heels clicking on the concrete floor. "Where did you go after the ceremony? I've been leaving you messages. Why haven't you been picking up?"

Because I've better things to do, because I've been at the hospital with my lover's son, because I can't stand listening to your incessant bullying.

She held her tongue. "Sorry, I…I've been busy."

Kat walked to the desk and pushed the newspapers to the side and leaned against the edge, next to Ariadne's purse.

"Well, Tammy asked me to give you this." Kat pressed a small manila envelope into her hand.

Spinning the paper in her fingers, Ariadne could feel something small and bulky inside, but the seal was still intact and she didn't want to open it in front of Katarina. She shoved it down into her purse. "Thanks."

Kat nodded and crossed her arms over her chest. "You left because you were busy? Too busy for honoring the goddess? That's a lie. Why did you leave us?"

"Epione called me away. I had to pray," Ariadne lied.

"Well, thanks to your little disappearing act, I had to clean up the ceremony without you. I mean, well, I got Tammy and Trina to help, but I basically had to manage the clean-up all by myself. I put Epione away in her normal place, but you need to clean her again."

So Kat doesn't really care that I'd left; only that she had to work… typical.

"Look, Kat, I'm tired. I haven't slept all weekend. Now isn't a great time for you to interrogate me; I have work to do." The moment the words fell from her lips, she knew she had made a mistake.

Kat's strangled squeak filled the air. "Who do you think you are? You don't *get back* to me. You answer me or may Epione damn you."

"I'm sorry, Kat. I didn't mean anything," she said humbly. "Like I said, I'm exhausted. I've been swamped."

Should I tell Kat about Captain Christos sniffing around?

Before Ariadne could continue, Kat interrupted. "Fine. I should've known."

"You should've known what?" Ariadne said, unable to control herself.

"You've always been so all-over-the-place when you meet a man you have feelings for. You even forgot to tell me about your little date at The Mouse Hole the other afternoon."

"Do you really think there is something between me and Dr. Morris?"

Kat pointed at the stack of papers. "I'm not the only one. I told you to keep an ear to the ground and keep track of what was happening at his site, not fuck him and attempt to kill Stavros."

Ariadne slammed her hands down on the desk. "I had nothing to do with the shooting."

Kat raised her dainty eyebrow and flashed a wicked smile. "I know."

Kat pushed herself off the edge of the desk and flattened her skirt down. She walked to the door and stopped. Turning around, she snickered and pointed at Ariadne's face. "By the way, you have ink right there on your forehead."

The door slammed shut.

Ariadne rubbed at her forehead. *Great. Just great. Like Kat needs more to hold above me.*

The door opened and Kat stuck her head back in. "Hey, has Stavros called you yet?"

Ariadne stopped rubbing and dropped her hands. "No. Why?"

"I'm surprised. He called me right away." Kat's gaze wandered to Ariadne's forehead and she snickered. "Anyway, he was discharged this morning from the hospital. Bunny and I are throwing him a party tonight at his place. You should stop by."

"Party? Yeah, maybe…" *What's Kat up to? Was she rubbing in the fact that I no longer have a place in Stavros' life? Or just that Stavros called her before me?*

Kat stared at her. "Bring your famous friend," Kat's words hung in the air. "Dr. Morris would just love to talk to Stav, I'm sure."

The door slammed behind her for a second time.

She walked out of her office and made her way to the lab to catalogue artifacts. The last time she had been in there had been with Kaden—and Beau. The boxes of artifacts she had shown Beau still sat out on the table, making Beau's presence stronger. Her heart clenched nervously in her chest. She couldn't escape any of her emotions and a tear slipped down her cheek. She had caused him so much pain.

Next to the box she had shown Beau was another bin. Opening the plastic lid of the bin, a ceramic bullhead stared back up at her. It made her think of Stavros.

Sliding the lid back on, she clicked the lid shut. Cataloging could wait.

Picking up the boxes, she put them away and tried to ignore the nagging pain in her chest. How was Kaden doing? How was Beau doing? He must have thought she was crazy. He had left her alone with his son for only a few minutes, and then she broke up with him. He must not have had a clue. Should she call him and check on Kaden?

No. It was best to wait. She needed to work, and come up with a way to clear her name. Until then, it was probably best to stay away from the man who the papers called "her new lover" and a motivation for attempting to murder her former flame.

She walked to the door and pushed the lock shut. There was only one thing that could take her mind off the catastrophe around her.

Walking back to the lab table, she opened up the doors, and kneeled down. Peering inside, she could only see a few boxes. Moving them out of the way, she reached into the back of the cabinet and found the button. She gave it a hard push. There was a slight click, followed by the whir of the cabinet rising up.

The stairway was exposed as the cabinet came to a stop above her. The lights flickered on as she walked to the top of the steps. It had been a long time since she had come to this place, since she needed answers she couldn't find within herself.

She stepped down the top few steps until she came to another switch. Pushing it, the cabinet slid back into place above her. The silence weighed down on her and made her heart race. Though she knew she was safe, the walls seemed to close in on her. She closed her eyes and offered a prayer.

Her shoes echoed off the concrete steps as she slowly made her way down the steep stairwell. Ten steps. Twenty. Thirty. The walls narrowed the farther she descended beneath the museum and sweat dampened her brow. *Why did they build these walls so close together?*

Stopping for a moment, she took a deep breath to calm her thrashing heart. *At least the stairs are well lit.*

She held the metal banister and forced her body to continue deeper. Another twenty steps. At last, her feet touched the level dirt of the temple floor. The sconces on the wall brought a warm light to the room as she walked through the marble columns at the room's entrance. Her feet scraped against the ground as she made her way between the chairs that sat in a perfect circle around the room.

The walls were covered in different images of their goddess. Her favorite was of Epione with her long black hair flowing in the winds, her crystal staff at her side, her feet resting in the water of the spring of life. The sick sat around her, their hands raised in supplication. For so long she had only understood their need. Now, with Kaden being sick, for the first time, she was empathetic to the gut-wrenching feeling of helplessness. How hard it must be for Beau to stand at his son's side and be able to do nothing but hold Kaden's hand and reassure him.

She approached the altar, where the glistening golden idol of Epione stood so tall it almost touched the ceiling. The ceremonial ceramic statue of Epione, from their festival, rested on its pedestal to the right of the larger idol. Kat had said she needed to clean it, but it looked immaculate. To the left of the statue was a silver dagger with a golden hilt where a scorpion glistened upon its pommel—a gift from their American cousin the veela, Gloriana Canis.

Ariadne stepped to the base of the statue, pressed her hand to her heart and bowed, but her eyes never strayed from her goddess. Epione's arms were akimbo as snakes wrapped around her arm. She kissed the goddess' toes and a surge of energy moved through her body from the idol. A feeling of calm filled her as she stepped back and lowered to her knees. She raised her arms and bowed until her forehead touched the ground.

"My goddess, I pray that you answer my prayers. I am in need of your help now more than ever."

A hiss sounded from above. Sitting up, she watched as the snakes upon the golden statue began to slither around Epione's arms. Their tongues flickered toward her and their eyes blinked from long hibernation.

A tingle rose from her arm. The black-inked snake on her flesh blinked its eyes and flickered its tongue like the golden snakes that looked down upon them.

"Are you here, my mother?" Ariadne's hands shook in her lap.

Was her mother going to finally answer her prayers?

The woman upon the altar shifted. Epione's arms lowered and caused the snakes to fall to the ground with a heavy clunk. Her mother's eyes fluttered open, the blue of her eyes a stark contrast to the shining golden eyelashes that surrounded them. Reverently, Ariadne dropped her gaze to the ground. "My mother…"

"Blessed be, sweet Ariadne."

Ariadne bowed.

"You do not need to bow to me. I am your sister as well as your goddess," Epione said, her voice soft and kind.

Ariadne sat up, but her gaze still focused on the dirt floor.

"Ariadne?"

"Yes, my goddess?"

"You must raise your eyes. Too often you look upon the ground and let others force you into submission."

Ariadne looked up as Epione sat down upon the altar.

"Thank you for coming to me, Ariadne. The ceremony was beautiful." Epione smiled. "I've long wanted to speak to you. I know the pain you have gone through, with Theseus and Dionysus. In fact, the god Dionysus talks of it often."

"Does he tell you how he hates me since I dismissed his love? How I should have ignored his philandering?"

"You don't have to accept less than you deserve. Just because Kat thinks you were wrong doesn't mean that you were. Standing up for what you believe is the most important thing one can do."

"Maybe, but just look at what happens when we do. We are cursed and hated." Ariadne stared at the goddess' golden smile.

Epione looked at her with pity. "The only person that hates you is you."

Ariadne snorted. "Tell Kat that."

"Kat has many issues, and you're right in assuming her dislike toward you, but hate is a strong word. You are an invaluable asset to Kat and her power struggles. Without someone to push down and assert her control upon, do you think she would still be the leader of your sisterhood?"

There was truth in her goddess' words, but was the situation really her fault? Had she allowed herself to be dominated?

Epione's eyes sparkled. "To help others, you must first help yourself—take control of your life, and fight for what you truly desire."

"If I go after my desires, people could die. My happiness is not worth such high a price."

The snakes slithered up Epione's legs and around her waist. They braided down her arms as she pushed herself to standing. Her arms rose as they had been. "My daughter, there are answers to the curse. However, you must be willing to fight."

"I'm willing to fight," Ariadne said almost defiantly.

"What about for your love Beau?" The goddess smiled.

Ariadne didn't know what to say. Yes, she had been feeling something, but love?

"Yes," Epione continued, "I've been watching how you act around him. He is a fine man. But he has many trials in his life."

Ariadne traced her finger over the snake on her arm. The snake's head turned to face her from her palm. "Going after the Labyrinth hasn't helped him."

Epione nodded. "No. But I believe it is you and Kat that have been adding to his tribulations."

Ariadne looked down to her feet, ashamed. "I only did what was ordered."

"I understand why you did it, but no longer can you take orders."

Ariadne stared up at the goddess. "But I can't let Beau find the Labyrinth or your crystal staff. We can't risk exposing ourselves to the humans."

The snakes slithered around Epione's arms. "It is true that many humans would use the staff for less than desirable endeavors, but there are many who would use it for good. Do you think that Beau is a man that would use it for anything other than noble purpose?"

Ariadne shook her head. "No, Beau is a good man."

Epione smiled brightly. "Then perhaps the problems lie within your sisterhood and not with the problems that humans would pose. There is someone who is hiding the truth. You must fight for what your heart desires. Find the truth."

Epione's eyes closed and her body stilled. The room went cold as her goddess' spirit lifted from the temple.

"Goodbye. And thank you, my goddess." A soft breeze fluttered against her cheek.

With some work, Ariadne would find the truth.

Ariadne stood and brushed the dust from her knees. She walked to the back of the temple and glanced back at the statue of Epione.

Her heart lightened. She would fight for her place and for what she truly desired—love. Beau was worth the fight. Love was worth the fight—even if it meant having to go against her sisters. She had to do what was right—she would follow her heart—and help Beau and Kaden.

Chapter Fourteen

The nurses had made a fuss about him not having physical contact with his son, but Beau didn't care. He wrapped his fingers around Kaden's limp hand as he watched the boy's chest move with shallow breaths as he slept. He loved him with every beat of his heart, and watching him wither away in the sterile cold hospital room was killing Beau as well.

He squeezed gently, giving Kaden love in the only way he could. He didn't want to wake him. What with the beeps of the monitors, the chattering of the nurses and alarms, it was a wonder the boy could sleep at all—he must be absolutely exhausted. A battle his body was fighting.

Kaden's face was pale green and deep purple bags were etched under his eyes. The sight was more than Beau could take. He stared at Kaden's limp hand. They were in this together. Whatever it took, no matter how long, Kaden would make it through this. He had to.

Kaden coughed in his sleep, the sound wet and choking. Beau squeezed tighter.

Come on, kid, fight this.

Beau shifted the mask on his face and leaned down and kissed the skin of his son's hand the same way he had done when Kae had been just a baby. He could still feel the weight of the newborn in his arms when the doctors had first forced him to hold his son. He had been so scared of something so small, so weak. Now here he was again, holding his son, feeling the weight of fear upon his shoulders.

Please God, help him fight this. Let me take his place. He doesn't deserve this. I'm the one who's let him down. I should've been there more for him. If I had just paid attention, maybe I could have stopped this from happening. Beau dropped his head and let it rest on the back of Kaden's hand.

He sat up and pulled the mask back over his mouth. The doctors would be upset if they saw him without it. He had promised to take care of himself. But what did they care? All they cared about was that the disease wouldn't spread. They didn't care that Kaden needed him, needed his love. The doctors didn't see Kaden for the young soft-hearted kid he was. But that was fine. All that mattered was that they concentrated on their job getting Kaden healthy.

There was a knock on the other side of the glass ICU window. The shades were pulled, so he dropped his son's hand and went to the door. A blonde woman, with her back turned to the window, stood on the other side.

"Can I help you?" Beau asked.

The blonde turned. Vickie, his student, smiled at him with a distinct look of pity on her face.

"Hi, Beau." She stared at him. He frowned. "I mean, Dr. Morris."

He stepped out of the isolation room, and pulled the mask from his face. "What are you doing here, Vickie? I thought you and the rest of the students were traveling around Crete for the next two weeks 'til you left for the states."

Her eyes followed his hand down and over his hospital gown. She looked back up. "I, er…heard about Kaden. I just couldn't stop from coming back and checking on you guys."

He pulled the blue latex gloves from his hands. The simple action flooded him with memories of Ariadne and her deception. He looked back up at the smiling, pretty blonde who stood before him.

I don't have time for women. But Vickie could be just a friend. Right? She had to know that I don't need a relationship, especially not one with a student.

"Thanks, Vickie. I appreciate you coming here. And Kaden'll be glad you came."

"I'm not here just for Kaden." She smiled seductively.

He looked away. "Look Vickie, I'm really flattered that you'd come back just to check on us."

"Well, it wasn't just to check on you. I thought you needed a woman to help. I heard your ex-wife was a no-show." Vickie slid her fingers into his. The hand felt out of place and a strange hollowness filled him.

He let his hand drop from hers. "You need to know that there could never be anything between me and one of my students."

Vickie reached out and touched his arm gently. "Dr. Morris, I don't think you understand. That's not what I'm after. I just want to be a *good* friend. That's all. But just so you know, I'd do anything for you."

Something in her inflection caught his attention, but just as he was about to ask what she meant, Dr. Dukakis walked through the swinging doors of the ICU. When the doctor saw him, Beau gave him a slight nod. The doctor frowned as he looked down at his clipboard and walked toward them.

"Please excuse me, Vickie. I need to talk to this gentleman." He motioned toward the white-lab-coated doctor.

She followed his gaze and nodded. "No problem, Beau. I'll be back." She turned and walked away, but she glanced back over her shoulder as she opened the door that led to the stairs.

He didn't know if he trusted that all she wanted was to be a friend, but he would take what he could get. Friends were in short supply.

The doctor walked up to him, clicking his blue pen as he always did. For a moment, Beau wondered if he always had the nervous tic or if it was just when it came to dealing with him and Kaden.

"Dr. Morris, I'm glad I caught you. We've received some results." The doctor looked down at the file. "Why don't you follow me?"

Dr. Dukakis led him to the farthest door in the long corridor labeled "Physicians Lounge" and pushed it open. The room was occupied with a large leather lounge chair and a table covered in antibacterial wipes, coffee carafes, paper cups, and sugar packets. A television was on, airing a television show with people talking in fast Greek.

Walking in, the doctor turned off the TV and motioned for Beau to sit at the brown laminate table.

Without a word, Beau sat down in a cheap hospital chair. The doctor sat in the leather chair across from him and opened the file.

"First of all, I know this has to be a challenge for you, not being from Crete and having a son in the hospital. If you need any help, please let me know and I can arrange for you to meet a therapist."

The doctor thinks I need a therapist? What, does he think I'm crazy?

Beau shook his head. "Thanks for the offer, but I think I'm all right."

"Great." The doctor nodded. "The reason I brought you in here is that we've received the lab results from his sputum test. We've run some cultures on the bacteria that we found and, looking at the early results, it appears that your son may be infected with XDR-TB. We can't say for sure for another five weeks, but in combination with what we've found, the state of his increasing symptoms, and his declining health, I would say with ninety percent certainty that we are dealing with XDR-TB."

Beau went numb. The doctor kept talking, but he couldn't hear the words, only see the movement of the man's mouth. Beau forced himself back into the moment. He needed to know exactly what he could do. "XDR-TB is what? Is it one of the treatable strains?"

The strain has to be treatable. It just has to.

The doctor cleared his throat. "I'm afraid it is the extensively drug resistant strain." He pulled at his tie. "But we are going to treat this as aggressively as we can. I'm going to start him on some second-line antibiotics as this strain is normally resistant to first-line therapies and see if we can get lucky."

"That's all you are going to do?" Beau asked. "Didn't you say it was resistant?"

The doctor flipped through the chart in his hands. "Like I said, maybe we can get lucky, but—"

"That's not enough," Beau growled. "There has to be something more to do than try to get *lucky*. This is my son. We'll do everything. It will work. Or I will find another doctor, one who can save him."

The doctor looked him in the eyes. "I'm so sorry. I appreciate your concern, but no other doctors can do more than what we plan to do. We'll do everything we can, but you need to start thinking about what any arrangements you would like to make. XDR-TB is usually a fast, prolific killer."

Beau clenched his fists until his hands shook, anything to make the pain of the doctor's words lessen, but no reprieve came. Kaden was sentenced to die.

Chapter Fifteen

The phone beeped from Ariadne's purse as she pulled the car into Stavros' long driveway.

Ignoring the phone, she drove past the guards with a wave. She parked at the valet stand and pulled the keys from the ignition. She opened her purse, and she saw the lit screen of her phone and the name she had been thinking of all day—Beau.

Why is he texting? There was no way he would ever forgive her for what she had done to his site.

She opened up the device and read the words: "Kaden not responding to antibiotics. Diagnosed with resistant strain. Thought you'd want to know."

She sank back into the driver's seat.

No…why is Zeus so cruel?

Her fingers pressed the buttons and the line connected. The phone rang, once, twice, three times. *Is Beau going to pick up? Or did he hate her so much that he never wanted to speak to her again?*

She pulled the phone away from her ear. A sound stopped her.

"Hello?" Beau's voice sounded drawn and tired.

"I got your text. Are you sure it's the antibiotic resistant strain?"

Beau exhaled as if she had deflated him. "The doctors said they'll try everything they can, but they told me not to expect much. They are hoping to get lucky, but I don't know."

Ariadne pushed her key back into the ignition. "I'll be there as soon as I can."

Beau sighed. "It's okay, Vickie is here."

Vickie? The overly flirtatious college student? Great. She's the last person he needed. He needs me.

"If you change your mind—"

"Thanks," he interrupted. "I gotta go." The line went dead.

She looked down at her phone. He had every right to be angry with her, but his dismissal didn't hurt any less.

The valet opened her door. "Good evening, Ms. Papadakis. Welcome."

She stared blankly at the young man as he offered his hand.

Her hand shook as she took the valet's arm.

"Are you okay, ma'am?"

She nodded, but she wasn't. How was she going to get Beau to forgive her?

The man helped her step out in her black floor-length dress. Her shoes pinched as she stepped away from her car, but she quickly forgot them as she looked up and saw the crowds of people through the open front door. Tonight she would make her goddess proud.

The valet handed her a ticket. Shoving the tiny piece of paper in her purse, she made her way up to the door of Stavros' seaside villa. Voices echoed from the house, and she stopped, taking a moment to still her thundering heart. She patted her hair and ran her hands down her black satin dress, smoothing invisible creases.

A car roared to a stop at the curb behind her and she looked back over her shoulder to watch as Captain Christos unbuckled his seat belt. He saw her, and waved. He jumped out of his car and rushed toward her. "I'm glad to catch you."

"Nice to see you too, Christos." She smiled. "How's the investigation going?"

He looked at her suspiciously. "I talked to Governor Kakos, and I have to admit, we haven't gotten any more leads."

An idea struck her and she wrapped her arm around the Captain's as she smiled at him seductively. "What would happen if Stavros dropped the charges?" Her voice sounded overly sweet, but the effect on the human was instantaneous as he softened beneath her touch.

He stared at her without blinking. "I… You…" She dropped her hand from his, but she couldn't help the wicked happiness that filled her. She still had *it*.

"Um…" Captain Christos blinked. "As you know, we've a *special* form of justice. If he wanted to make the charges disappear, well, they probably would."

She smiled.

"But I doubt that the governor is going to let a shooting slide." Christos reached out to touch her.

Her stomach tightened with the excitement caused by his words. She ignored his outstretched hand and instead let her fingers trail up Christos' arm. A pulse of lust radiated from his body. "Many people own guns here." He stared down at her fingers as she spoke. "It would be impossible to find out who was behind the shooting. Don't you think?"

His eyes were glazed over with desire. "You're probably right, but well, it's the governor's choice."

"I completely understand, Christos," Ariadne said, her voice soft. "But I'm sure the governor doesn't want to waste any more of your time."

He nodded as he stared blankly at her. "Yeah. Sure. You're probably right," he said dazedly.

Human men are so easy.

She dropped her fingers from his flesh, and sadness crept upon his face. "Let's head in, shall we?"

He nodded.

The orchestra was playing a Bach piece as the butler opened the door and motioned them inside. She left Christos standing alone as she made her way into the party. A group of people from the museum's board of trustees looked up at her and waved in recognition.

Stavros had his back against the bar where he leaned with an air of arrogance, an almost empty crystal tumbler in his hand. When he saw Ariadne enter the foyer, he smiled and waved her over with a tilt of his head and a lift of his glass.

Kat wiggled through the crowd and grabbed her arm. "Do you really think you should be seen talking to him right now?"

Her forced smile faded as she looked down at Kat's spindly fingers. "I will make my own choices, but thank you for your concern."

Kat dropped her arm and stared at her in shock. After a moment, she glared. "You know it's funny. Trina said the same thing. Now look at where she is."

"What are you talking about?"

Kat smirked. "Trina had to fall for that boy. She wouldn't listen when I told her to leave him alone. Now that the kid's almost dead, she realized she should've listened. She's just lucky that I found her."

"What are you talking about?"

"Oh, didn't you hear?" Kat said in a whisper. "Trina was caught with her shed skin this morning, trying to commit suicide."

"What?"

Poor Trina. And poor Kaden. Hopefully no one had told him, he didn't need any more stress.

Kat picked an invisible thread from the shoulder of Ariadne's dress. "That's what happens when you mess with trying to love. Hopefully *others* will use this as an example of how not to behave."

She pulled away from Kat's fingers. "How I live my life and the choices I make are no longer any of your concern."

"Don't you dare forget who I am. I saved the staff. Epione will strike you down if you go against me," Kat whispered through gritted teeth, giving her the crazed look of a rabid jackal. "Did you forget your place?"

With a tight smile, Ariadne pulled her arm from Kat's grip. "I'm making a new one."

Kat's neck bulged and her face reddened. Ariadne's heart was in her throat. Before Kat could pull herself together, Ariadne made her way across the packed room.

She smiled and nodded at the greetings she received as she brushed past familiar faces. She ignored the urge to look back at the woman who would now stop at nothing to ruin her.

Stavros placed his glass down on the marble bar, stepped toward her and offered her his embrace. Stopping short of stepping into his arms, she extended her hand. There was a look of shock upon his face, but he recovered quickly and instead lifted her hand to his lips, and gave it a quick peck. "I'm glad you made it. I wasn't sure you would come. After, well, you know."

"I couldn't miss your homecoming. Not after Kat's gracious invitation."

"I'm sorry, I meant to call, but—"

She stopped him with a wave of the hand. "Thank you for your apology, but it's unnecessary. I shouldn't have been so upset at the hospital. You just caught me at an off moment."

"Are you feeling better?"

"In a matter of speaking, but there is work that needs to be done. Work that I'm going to need your help with."

Stavros laughed. "So this is why you came? You don't really care about me at all, do you?"

At the sound of his laugh, Bunny sauntered to his side and slipped her arm through the crook of his. "Oh hello, Ariadne, I'm so glad you're here." Her voice trilled with the phony felicitates. "We were just talking about you." Bunny eyed Stavros with distinct ownership.

Ariadne's smile flickered for only a moment at Bunny's pronouncement of "we." Of course, Bunny would lay claim to the man who had only weeks before refused public acknowledgment that the flake even existed.

Looking at Stavros, she noticed him cringe. It was nice to see that he identified exactly how ridiculous he must appear to her.

"I'm sure you were saying just the *nicest* things," Ariadne said, as she glared at the bottle-blonde woman. "If you wouldn't mind, Stavros and I were talking."

Bunny's jaw dropped.

"Besides, I'm sure there is a desk somewhere that needs a good shining." Ariadne beamed.

Bunny jerked her arm out of Stavros' arm. "You—"

"Bunny," Stavros said sternly. "Why don't you go see if your friends have arrived? I'm sure they are looking for you."

Ariadne snickered as Bunny turned and stomped away.

Stavros grabbed her hand and led her away from the bar and toward the private kitchen. Walking in, he dropped her hand, walked to the refrigerator and pulled out a bottle of water. Opening it, he guzzled it down.

"Sure, I would take one of those," Ariadne said, perturbed at his usual rudeness.

Dropping the bottle from his lips, he wiped away a drip of water that trailed from his oversized lips. "What's going on with you?"

"What are you talking about? I just want a water." She motioned at the fridge.

"Okay." He opened the door and grabbed another bottle and thrust it at her, but he eyed her suspiciously. "What was the business you wanted to talk to me about?"

"I want you to reopen Dr. Morris' site." Her words hung in the air. "And call the police off of your shooting."

He sat the plastic bottle down on the concrete counter. He ran his fingers over the stubble of his chin. "You can't expect that I am going to let whomever was responsible for the attempted assassination go, do you?"

"That's not what I'm asking. You can still find out who did it and take care of it *in another fashion*. I'm just asking you to call the police off. They won't allow Dr. Morris' site to be reopened while they are still investigating."

"I see." He smiled wickedly. "But aren't you and Kat worried about what he'll find in the Labyrinth?"

She stiffened. "That's for me to worry about."

A smile flickered on his lips. "I have to say, I think I like this new you."

"I'm glad, because this's what you'll be getting from here on out."

His eyebrows shot up. "I know what it must be like for you to see me with Bunny and all, but if you're still interested, we could work things out. I need a strong woman, and the people would love this attitude you are displaying."

"Would you love me, Stavros?"

He threw his head back as he laughed. When she didn't stir, he stopped and looked at her. "Oh, you were being serious?"

She looked away from him and down to the bottle in her hands.

"We both know that's out of the question," Stavros began. "Love is such a useless emotion. We get along so much better without any of that. I like our arrangement, our mutual respect."

"Since when have you respected me, Stavros?"

A quick flash of humility played upon his face, but was quickly replaced with his usual distant expression. "I can change, Ariadne. I'll make it better for you. I admit, I haven't been the best boyfriend in the world, but I thought we were both on the same page with everything."

"We weren't."

He reached out for her. "If you take me back, I promise I'll stop seeing other women."

She had waited for decades for him to utter those words, but now that they fell from his lips, she just sighed. It was too late for them to be together, she had grown past trusting him. He would always be just a bull, taking what he wanted regardless of others' feelings; she had more than her share of evidence.

When she didn't move toward him, he dropped his hands.

"Listen, Stav, I just need you to do what I asked. I don't want to get back into our old rut. You're great, but you're not for me. I need something more, something better."

"What? And you think you are going to find that with a poor American archeologist?"

Opening the water bottle, she pressed it to her lips and swallowed a sip. Slowly, she twisted the lid back and sat the bottle gently next to Stavros' on the counter. "You don't need to worry about who I'm interested in. All you need to know is that it'll no longer be you. So you can fuck whomever, whenever you want. You don't have to pretend to hide it from me any longer. I no longer give a shit about your escapades."

Stavros bristled. "If you are thinking that talking to me like this is going to get your *boyfriend's* little site opened back up, you are sorely mistaken."

She stepped toward him and ran her finger up the black satin lapel of his tuxedo jacket all the way to the white bandage on his neck. Tracing her finger around the edge, she found the pricking thread of the plastic stitches and pressed her nail into them. "You will open the site."

Stavros grimaced and pulled away from her hand. "What the hell do you think you're doing? You have no authority to boss me, or anyone else."

"Oh, really?" She threatened. "I believe I do." She opened her purse and pulled out an envelope. "Inside you will find a flash drive filled with pictures of you and your brother, Nico, doing all kinds of sexually perverse things. Him more than you, but I have to admit I was a little shocked with the quantity of women you were with in some of the photos. How could you satisfy so many when you struggled to satisfy me?"

He grabbed the envelope from her hands and ripped it open. He dumped the flash drive into his hand and glowered at it, as if he could make it and its contents magically disappear. "You wouldn't dare use this against me."

"Not that one in particular. I have another copy, don't worry." She smiled. "Now, I don't want to have to use any of these. Seeing them once was more than enough for me. You and I have had some great times together and I don't want to have to take things to the next level. I would appreciate it if we could still be friends, but I'm no longer under anyone's control."

He nodded as he curled his fingers around the black plastic rectangle that was filled with evidence of his character. "Friends. Okay." He dropped the flash drive to the floor. "We will never speak of what is on this drive again." He brought the heel of his gleaming patent leather shoe down. There was the crack of plastic as the flash drive broke.

"Agreed. But with the understanding that Beau's site is reopened and Christos and his men are called off."

"Fine." Stavros twisted his foot in the other direction.

Leaning in, she pressed her lips to the smooth skin of his cheek. "Thanks, Stav. Without you, I would've never realized how much power I truly possessed."

He pulled back and looked down at her with a look of disbelief upon his face.

Ariadne turned and strode out, leaving him alone in the soulless kitchen.

She pushed past the throngs of people that packed into Stavros' mansion. Officer Christos waved at her and motioned for her to come over, but Ariadne shook her head. She needed out of the mess of people, away from the politics, and perfume-tainted air. Kat was nowhere to be seen, but her absence wasn't the relief she would have expected.

Walking out of the foyer and onto the almost empty patio, she reached down and opened her purse and extracted the parking stub, when she was met with Tammy's voice. "Did Kat give ya the pictures?"

"What are you doing here, Tammy?"

Tammy scanned the area. "I knew ya'd be here. And I needed to speak to ya without Kat knowin'. Did ya get them pictures?"

"I did," Ariadne said, as she handed her stub to the parking attendant. "But how did you get them?"

Tammy's gaze shifted around as if she feared seeing someone or something. "Before I had Ivan, I had an investigator following Nico. Stavros just happened to be there most of the time. And I thought ya should know the kinda man that ya had in your life."

"Thanks," Ariadne said wearily. "Where's Ivan tonight?"

"Oh, he went back to the States. His wife was missing him. I only came because I needed to see you. I don't like being this close to the bull, Stavros."

"Did you have something to do with the shooting? What's going on, Tammy?"

Tammy looked around nervously. "I just heard about Kaden and I thought maybe I could be a help. I tried to get in to see 'em, but I couldn't get by the nosey wards." She opened up her purse for Ariadne to see the brown vials and bug-filled jars inside. "I even brought some stuff that might be useful. Do ya think ya can get me in?"

"I think so, but how did you hear about Kaden?"

"Oh, everyone is talking about the curse and the boy. But Kat's the one who told me about it."

"What did Kat want with Kaden?" Ariadne asked.

Tammy pulled a bottle of green sludge from her pocket and swallowed the contents down. "She wanted me to poison him, like I did Nico."

Chapter Sixteen

The revolving glass doors of the hospital circled with a monotonous whir and click as Ariadne and Tammy approached the entrance.

"We need to heal him. Do you think you can really help?" Ariadne asked the witch.

Tammy opened her giant khaki-colored purse and reached inside. Glass clinked and there was a sound like beads being shaken as the witch rifled through the contents. "Well, I can give it a try. I don't have a lotta stuff to work with, but I'll see what I can do."

"Well that's better than nothing. Kaden is such a great kid. He just got mixed up with the wrong crowd."

"Ya mean y'all?" Tammy asked with marked pity in her voice.

"Unfortunately, yes." Ariadne's black gown clung to her legs as she led the way through the maze of sterile white halls. "His room's right around the corner. I'll get Beau out of the room while you do whatever it is you need to do. But you won't have much time."

She grabbed a mask and gown off the isolation cart outside of Kaden's door and put them on over her clothes. "Tammy, why don't you wait here? I'll be out in a second, and then you can go in."

Tammy nodded and walked toward the nurse's station.

Vickie was sitting at the foot of the bed while Beau sat next to the window. Beau's eyes were closed, but as she walked in, his eyes opened.

Kaden was attached to a ventilator and there was the hum and whoosh of the machine as it kept the boy alive. Kaden was asleep and tubes ran out of his nose, mouth, and arms. She blanched as she took in how much the boy had deteriorated since the last time she had been there. It wouldn't be long if something wasn't done.

"Ariadne?" Beau said in a ragged voice. "I thought you weren't coming."

"I'm sorry, but I had to talk to you." She looked over at Vickie. "Hi, Vickie. It's nice to see you again."

Vickie gave her a confused look. "Hey."

Ariadne tried to hold her tongue, but failed. "I thought you would've gone back to your parents by now."

It was hard to see Vickie's response through her blue surgical mask, but Ariadne caught a flicker of anger in her eyes. "I had to stay and take care of the boys. They mean a lot to me."

"I'm glad to hear it. *They* need as much support as they can get right now."

Beau sat up and rubbed the sleep from his eyes. "We don't want to disturb Kae."

Ariadne's cheeks flushed. She had no intention of a verbal discord with a lumbering college girl. She was better than this. And if Beau wanted the girl more than he wanted her, that was his choice. Though she would fight for him, if his heart led him toward the blonde harlot the only thing she could do to bring him back would be to seduce him, and there was no real lasting love in such a tempestuous foundation.

Kaden's IV beeped. His face was pale and swollen.

Maybe it was better that Beau would go for the girl; loving a nymph came at too high a cost.

"Why don't we take a break and get some coffee or something?" Beau stood up and stretched. "You coming, Vickie?"

Vickie looked up at Beau with a slight grimace. "Sure, it would be nice to get up and walk."

Ariadne led the way out of the room. Looking down the hall, she stripped off the isolation gown and mask, but Tammy had disappeared. Hopefully the witch would notice their absence.

Beau and Vickie threw their clothes in the biohazard laundry and Beau walked up beside her. They made their way to the elevator, forcing Vickie to walk behind them. Ariadne nervously tapped her foot until the door opened and they quietly made their way toward the garlic-scented cafeteria.

Beau stared at Ariadne, his eyes were red and his face was covered in stubble. He opened the cafeteria's door for her and bumped into Vickie as she moved to walk through after her. "Sorry," Beau mumbled.

Vickie frowned. "Why don't you guys just talk? I'll come back later."

"You—"

"That'll be great," Ariadne said, stopping Beau from finishing his sentence.

Vickie glared at her, then looked at Beau. "I'll meet you back up in the room in a few minutes. Okay?"

Beau stared at her for a few seconds. "Why don't you go back to your host family? I'll call you. Visiting hours are almost over." He looked down at his watch.

Vickie stepped back, looking affronted. "But... You..." she stammered. "If that's what you want, Beau."

"Yeah," Beau said, as he looked up from his watch. "Please."

Vickie nodded, and without addressing Ariadne, turned around and walked out of the cafeteria.

Getting their coffees, Ariadne and Beau sat down at a melamine table with a white vase filled with plastic yellow flowers.

"Thank you." Ariadne thumbed the lip of the paper coffee cup.

Beau looked up at her. "For what?"

"For talking to me. I know how upset you must be right now. But you have to trust that I didn't do what I did to hurt you."

He rubbed his hands over his face and then dropped them to the table. "I just don't understand it. I don't understand why you would want to shut us down. We did nothing to you. We are only helping the museum in the long run."

"I know. You're right. But I don't just work for the museum." She paused and took a sip of her coffee.

"Who else do you work for? The NSF?" He leaned away from her and crossed his arms over his chest.

Her anger was palpable. "Why would I be working for the NSF?"

"They pulled my funding right after I met you. It's just a little bit strange that everything bad that has been happening has gone down since you made an appearance into our lives."

"I know." Her heart clenched. He was never going to forgive her for what she'd done. "But I have a feeling that you are about to get lucky."

He snorted. "Well, things couldn't get much worse. All I'm hoping for is that Kaden gets better."

"I do have some good news for you. And know it's not about Kae." *Though I am working on that.* She smiled. "But I just talked to Stavros."

"Is that what's going on with your get-up?" He pointed at her black evening gown. "You had a hot date?"

"No, no." Ariadne flattened the fabric. "We definitely didn't have a hot date, it was better."

Beau looked at her with a confused expression on his face. "What do you mean it was better than a *hot date*?"

She blushed. "Don't worry. I have no interest in having sex with that man. Don't worry about that."

Beau looked down. "It's up to you whether or not you want to have a relationship with him or anyone else."

"I don't want a relationship with him." She gave him a furtive glance. "There's only one person I want to have a relationship with, but I think he's already taken."

He looked out the window. "I know how that goes."

Didn't he understand? Or is he trying to avoid my inference?

"I...uh..." She twisted her hands. "I came here to let you know some great news about your site."

"Did it burn down?" He sat forward and dropped his hands to the table.

She laughed, the sound echoed off the apathetic walls. "Um, no. Stavros has decided to reopen it, without the tourists."

"What? But how? What about the investigation?" Beau stammered.

She placed her hand on his, half-expecting him to pull away, but he didn't. Instead, he looped his thumb over hers. "In the next few days, you can go back to your work. The investigation will no longer be a concern."

Beau's shoulders fell. "I can't leave Kaden. I can't leave him while he's sick."

"He'll get better soon. Didn't you say the doctors were going to try more meds?"

He nodded weakly.

"You just need to trust that everything will work out."

I'm on it. I'm doing almost everything I can do, she thought as she entwined her fingers with his. "Kaden is sleeping, right?"

He nodded.

She stroked his skin. "Why don't I take you back to your apartment and you can get a shower and take a nap? If you want, I can come back and sit with him until you're rested."

He stared at her hand. "I don't want to leave him."

"I know. But you need a break." She tried to smile.

He was silent for a minute. "Let me tell Kaden where I'm going."

The ventilator whooshed and wheezed as it pushed and pulled air from Kaden's body. Aside from the vast array of machines, the room was empty. *Had Tammy even been in?*

Kaden's color did look a bit pinker. Glancing at the medley of machines, she noted that his blood pressure had risen. Could Tammy be responsible for the better numbers?

Beau walked up next to the head of the bed and lifted Kaden's hand to his lips. Never before had she seen such an honest and tender expression of love. He must have been so afraid, so absolutely terrified that his son wouldn't make it. Her heart broke for them.

Ariadne turned away to hide the tears that welled in her eyes. "Excuse me, I'll be right back."

Walking out of the room, she made her way down the hall and into the stairwell. She just needed a moment. It was important that she stay strong for Beau and Kaden, he didn't need a weakling around him. He needed someone who could help bear the burden of the curse. And she and Trina were responsible.

Had Beau heard about Trina?

It was better to let it go, he didn't need another thing to deal with right now. Besides, if Kat found Trina, the situation was under control. There was no way Kat would let one of her loyal subordinates die; if she did, her hierarchy would be in danger. She loved power and control too much to let the death of a young nymph jeopardize what she held so dear.

A tap on her shoulder broke her concentration. Instinctively, her hands balled into tight fists and she spun around.

"I've been waiting for ya." Tammy peered around her and down the stairs. They were alone. "I did what I could for the poor kiddo. He's doing better, but I gotta say, it don't look real good."

Ariadne dropped her hands. "If I got you more supplies, do you think it would help?"

"I don't know."

"You're a witch. There has to be something more that you can do," Ariadne choked, as a tear slipped down her cheek.

Tammy put her hand on Ariadne's shoulder and squeezed. "I'm gonna try. But we won't really know 'til tomorrow if anything's gonna work. Be patient. I'll do my best. But you guys need to get outta here so I can get some time to work before visiting hours are over. I'll let ya know how it goes."

Ariadne opened the door. "Thanks, Tammy. I appreciate it."

*

The shower shut off with a loud thump and a bang. The sound perfectly matched the rest of Beau's dingy apartment. Ariadne sat at the desk and listened as the sounds of Beau's grunts filtered out into the bathroom.

"You okay in there?"

"Yep. Old, but great," Beau called back.

He didn't have a clue what old *was.*

"Oh, shit," Beau grumbled.

"What? Did you fall down and break a hip, old man?"

"Ha ha ha, real funny. No. I forgot my clothes."

Without meaning to, she smiled. "Don't let me stop you from coming out to get them."

The door cracked open. "I don't know about most Greeks, but this place doesn't seem to believe in towels that cover."

She laughed. "If you want, I'll look away." She turned her head slightly to the side, but kept an eye on him as the door moved wider.

"That's not really looking away," he said, with a tired, but playful edge to his voice.

She turned and looked directly at him as he walked out of the bathroom. Water dripped down his tan sculpted chest. How had she forgotten how good he had looked in the moonlight? He held the small bath towel tightly, which made his biceps look more pronounced. She sucked in a breath as she felt the wetness grow between her thighs.

"You okay?" He smiled, but his eyes were weary.

"Sorry. I…" She looked away. "You need to get your rest. I shouldn't have stayed this long." She rose from her chair and stepped toward the door, but he grabbed her.

"Stop. I want to thank you for whatever it was that you did to make Stavros reopen the site. I know how hard it is dealing with an ex. I still don't know why you did what you did to my site, but I'm sure you had your reasons."

"I'm so sorry, Beau. Know that I never wanted to hurt you. I never *want* to hurt you. It was a mistake. One that I'm trying to fix."

Still holding his towel, he stepped toward her. He pushed a stray hair behind her ear, and his warm hand fell to her waist. "I know."

His wet, warm breath brushed against her skin, and made her heart quicken. She lifted her chin and met his gaze. The subtle light made the brown of his eyes even more mesmerizing. He leaned in, she moved slightly forward, and their lips met.

The sound of his towel hitting the floor was the only noise besides the thundering of her heart. He grabbed her hips and pulled her into his nakedness. He pressed against her, and her inner nymph took over as she rolled her body against him. She sucked on his bottom lip until he moaned.

She pulled back, releasing his mouth. "This isn't resting."

"No, but I need this just as badly. I need to know that you still care about me." He ran his fingers up her back as she sucked in an excited breath. "I've never felt more alone. I just want a few hours of something good."

She rested her head on his chest. "You aren't alone anymore," she whispered. "I want you in my life. And I want to be a part of your life. Can you forgive me for the things I have done?"

He kissed her forehead and down her face to her lips. She yielded to his searching tongue.

Leading her to the bed, he unzipped the back of her dress. She let it slip down her shoulders, revealing the tops of her breasts. Beau kissed the bottom of her neck, over her collarbone and down between her naked breasts, making the tingling need between her thighs grow. He pulled her into his mouth and sucked. The feeling of his tongue flicking against her nipple made her knees grow weak. Beau must have realized, because he let go and laid her on the bed.

"You're so unbelievably sexy. I don't know how I ever got this lucky to have you share my bed." He pulled the black dress down past her waist. She lifted her hips and he eased it from her body and dropped the fabric to the floor.

Sitting up, she took his hand. "I'm the lucky one."

She led his fingers to the top of her black lace panties. He needed no coaxing as he slipped his finger under the waist, tugged them downward, and revealed all of her. He dropped his knees to the floor and pushed her knees apart.

He put his mouth on her and moved in rhythm with the arching of her body. He hummed and her body contorted with the intense sensation. The tempo of his pulse increased.

"Oh, goddess." She forced her body to sit up.

Beau stopped. She pulled him on the bed next to her, climbed on top of his strong body and led him inside of her with the movement of her hips. He reached up and took hold of her body as she rotated her hips, driving him deeper inside of her wetness. He thumbed her nipple as their bodies moved in perfect unison.

The sweat dampened her breasts and a droplet slid down her flesh. Beau smiled and kissed away the drip. Without removing himself, he gently moved her onto her back and took control. The simple action drove her to the edge. "I'm close," she moaned.

"Come for me." He drove deeper.

She closed her eyes as she felt the precipice nearing. Her toes curled as her body quivered and writhed beneath him as the wave of pleasure swept through her body. His body mimicked hers as he shuddered and moaned. Holding her close, his head fell to her chest and their heavy breaths mirrored each other.

Her phone chirped from her purse on the desk, but the sound barely registered through her fog of euphoria.

He leaned down and tickled the skin of her neck with his lips.

Laughing, she pushed him off. He smiled as he moved onto the bed beside her.

Beau trailed his fingers down her body. He picked up her arm and ran his finger over the black ink of her snake. "What are these tattoos for?"

"I belong to a group. They are our symbol."

"Snakes are your thing?" He put his finger in her palm on top of the snake's eye.

"Sort of, yeah. I can't talk much about it."

"So you are in a secret group?" He sat up on his elbow. "I'm intrigued."

Smiling seductively, she took his fingers from her palm and led them to the intersection of her thighs, in blatant avoidance of his question.

"You can't be ready again," he scoffed, as he took the bait.

"You would be surprised." She pushed his hand in a slow circle as a smile danced across his face. "If you don't think you can go again yet, we can wait."

He laughed. "I'm a man, not a god."

She pulled his hand away and sat up. "I'm glad you're not. You're better than that."

Beau smirked as he laid his head on the pillow and motioned for her to come closer to him. She obliged and wrapped her body around his and laid her head on his sweat-dampened chest. His heart slowed as she lay silently taking in the moment.

"Ariadne?"

"Hmm?"

"Have you ever wanted kids?"

For a moment, she lay there in stunned silence, trying to think of the right thing to say. "I've never really thought about it."

"You're a woman. You have to have thought about it at some point or another."

She lifted her head and gazed up at him. "That's a broad

statement to make. Have you ever thought that maybe I'm not like other women?"

"I know you're nothing like other women. But, I mean, haven't you ever wanted to get married and raise a family? You're so beautiful. And you were with Stavros for a long time. Why didn't you go down that road?"

Her heart fell. "There are a lot of reasons Stavros and I never had kids. I mean, can you imagine him as a father?" She mentally shuddered. "No, wait. Don't think about him as a father."

"That's it? He just wasn't 'dad' material?"

She sighed resignedly. "No. I can't have children. So it was never really an option for me."

Beau looked stunned. "I'm sorry. I shouldn't have asked."

"Do you want more children?"

He sat back and looked up at the ceiling. "Truthfully, I've thought about it. More kids would be nice, but I failed so badly with the first one. I mean, I'm never around. I'm always working out in the field or in the lab. It's hard to raise a kid when you aren't there."

"You're a great dad. I don't know what you're talking about."

He ran his hands up and down the bare skin of her back. "You're wrong. I stayed away from that kid when he was small. It's my biggest regret. If I could do it all again, I would've probably still gotten the divorce, but I would've stuck around, instead of running."

"Sometimes you run away from things, thinking it's better than fighting, but it's hard to tell in the moment. I'm sure you did what you thought was right."

"Not right so much as necessary. I had to pay child support, but I was just getting done with my PhD. No one was hiring where we'd been living, and Lynda wasn't willing to move. But I had to pay the bills. I had to support him in the only way I could."

"I understand. We all try to act as we think we should. Trust me, we all have our secrets."

I only understand too well. There were so many regrets. Loving bad men. Theseus. Dionysus. Walking away when I should have stood strong. And I can never tell him how much we have in common. She lifted his hand and kissed the back of his fingers.

Ariadne rolled her body fully on top of Beau. Her hand strayed downward and she tried to tell him that she empathized in the only way she could.

Chapter Seventeen

Tammy's telephone message kept replaying in Ariadne's mind. *Kaden isn't doing good. I tried but…*

The witch had done everything she could, but the curse of the nymphs was more powerful than a simple witch's magical abilities. Zeus was a fickle bastard.

Beau was gowned up and had pulled the mask down over his face. She followed him into Kaden's room. A Greek Orthodox priest was standing in the corner of the room wearing black robes and a cylindrical black hat, covered by the sterile hospital gown, latex gloves, and a mask.

He waved slightly as they entered the room. "Hello, Dr. Morris and Miss…"

"Papadakis," she offered.

The priest nodded. "Katarina called me last night about your son. She was concerned about his health. I wish to give him anointment." The priest looked down at Kaden and frowned. "He needs to be prepared for the Lord."

Beau stepped between the priest and his son. "Get the hell out of here, Kat doesn't know what she's talking about. He's not going to die. He's going to be fine. The doctors said we're going to get lucky." He pointed at Ariadne. "She says we're going to get lucky. He's going to live. He doesn't need you. He only needs some goddamned drugs that work!"

The priest's eyes widened at Beau's outburst. "I understand your pain, my son, but we must do what is right for our Lord."

"He's not my Lord. My Lord wouldn't allow this to happen to my son."

Ariadne stepped beside Beau and put her hand on his arm. She could feel him shaking with anger. She leaned into his ear. "It's only Kat's game. She's malicious and is trying to make a point to me that she's in control," she whispered. "Kaden is very sick, but I think I have a way we can save him."

"What?" Beau stared at her.

She shook her head, as she tried to urge him to keep his voice lowered.

"Do the unction, Father." She motioned toward Kaden.

Beau stepped away and let the priest move to the bedside, but his eyes remained on Ariadne.

The priest pulled a bottle of holy oil from his robe and placed the sacrament on Kaden's forehead. He said a prayer quietly in Greek. She could still feel Beau's eyes on her.

The priest laid his gloved hand on Kaden's arm and looked back at them. "It is done."

"Thank you, Father." Ariadne bowed respectfully.

"You are welcome, my friends." The priest walked to Beau and took his hand. "May God be with you and your son. I know that you are hurting, but God will do what is right."

"Like killing my son?" Beau growled.

The priest looked at him with pity upon his face. "Trust in God."

Beau jerked his hand from the priest's and walked to the window. He kept his back to them as he stared out into the early morning sky.

There was a knock on the door. They all turned and stared as a gowned, masked, and gloved Trina walked in. Her eyes were swollen and red and a tear rested on her cheek. "Ariadne?"

"Hello, Trina. What're you doing here?"

"I'm sorry I haven't come before. It's just...been...been so hard," she stammered, as she dabbed at her eyes with a tissue.

"If you'll excuse me," the priest said, as he made his way out of the room.

"Why was the priest here?" Trina asked with marked fear in her voice.

Beau had a scowl on his face.

"Let's step out really quick, Trina." Ariadne motioned her back toward the door.

Trina glanced at Beau and nodded.

The priest was gone when they stepped out into the hallway. Nurses bustled around the corridor, but none seemed to be paying them any attention.

"I heard about what you tried to do," Ariadne whispered.

Trina stared at the floor. "Kat told you, didn't she?"

"Why did you do it?"

Fresh tears glistened in Trina's eyes. "What else could I do? Kaden is dying and it's all my fault. I knew I shouldn't love, but I didn't listen to the sisterhood about the curse. He was just so great. I couldn't help it."

Ariadne looked back at the room where Beau stood waiting. "I get it. You can't help who you fall in love with."

Trina nodded.

"Kaden's very sick. I had Tammy in here and she tried to help, but it didn't work. There's only one thing left to do. But it means that we'll be exiled from our group forever. If you don't want to help me, I completely understand."

Trina stared in at Kaden. "What do you want to do?"

Ariadne looked around the hall to make sure no one was listening. "I'm going to go to the Labyrinth and try to find Epione's crystal staff."

Trina frowned. "That's only a myth, isn't it?"

"No, it exists. Kat put it in there the night we were cursed."

"What about Beau? What are you going to tell him?"

The door opened. "Tell me what?" Beau stuck his head out.

Shit.

"Nothing."

Beau stepped out of the room and crossed his arms over his chest. "Don't lie to me."

"Let's just take him with us," Trina argued. "We're gonna need him."

Ariadne glanced at Beau. "You might be right. We'll need all the help we can get. There are things down there that aren't even welcome in the world of Hades."

"If this has anything to do with helping Kaden, I'm willing," Beau said. "But you need to tell me what's going on."

Ariadne's stomach churned with nerves. "Okay, but we need to hurry. Before it's too late."

Beau pulled the gown off and threw the mask and gloves in the trash. They followed his lead. Rushing down the hall, they ran to her car.

Slamming the passenger door shut, Beau looked at her. "What's going on? Where are we going?"

She put the key in the ignition, and roared the car to life. Squealing the tires, they rushed out of the parking lot and toward Gournai.

Beau stared at her. "You need to talk to me, Ariadne."

There was no avoiding it any longer. "You know how we were talking last night and I told you I was in a secret group?"

"Of course, how could I forget? Are you in a mercenary group or something? Are you really the one behind the governor's shooting?"

"I had nothing to do with that. Unfortunately, the sisterhood might have. I think Kat'll stop at nothing to stop people from getting to the Labyrinth and what's inside."

"Is that why you shut down my site? Because I'm close to the Labyrinth?" he said in a choked voice. "I'm close?"

"Too close. That's why Kat forced my hand. We had to shut it down."

"You tried to stop me from accomplishing my dream because Kat wanted you to?" He looked at her with disgust.

"Don't look at me like that. It wasn't my decision. She's the leader. For a long time I've been just a member—a very low-ranking member."

He glared at her. "Who are you?"

She pointed at Trina in the back seat. "She and I are sisters of sorts. We are Nymphs. We can seduce and bewitch men. A couple of thousand years ago we were struck with a curse from Zeus. Nymphs will never experience lasting true love. If we fall in love, our lovers are fated to die a tragic death." She glanced in the mirror back at Trina as she drove down the road.

He sat in stunned silence.

Say something, she silently begged.

Beau tapped his fingers on the door. "So if a man falls in love with you, he will die?"

She gripped the wheel tight, as if she let go she would lose control of her teetering emotions. "That's what they say. I think that's what happened between Kaden and Trina."

He turned and addressed Trina. "Did Kaden love you?"

From the rearview mirror, Ariadne watched as Trina nodded. "I love him more than you can know."

Beau looked back at Ariadne. "Trust me, I think I can relate."

There's no way he is talking about me. He doesn't love me. He can't love me. He won't love me, not after knowing the disaster love causes. Oh please, no.

There was a tense silence. "Do you have anything in the car that we could use for weapons?" Beau said, as he opened the glove compartment and shuffled through the miscellaneous papers.

"What?" Ariadne asked. "Why?"

"Well, if the Labyrinth is filled with all these *worse-than-Hades* things, then don't you think we should at least be prepared?"

Ariadne turned the car off the highway and back toward the museum. "You're right, and I think I know something that might be useful. Do you think you can keep a secret?"

Chapter Eighteen

Ariadne had tried to explain it to him that it was unlikely anything was still alive in the Labyrinth, but she wasn't hard to convince that they needed weapons, which made him worry that there was more than what she had confessed.

He had to grip the handle of the car as she whipped into the empty parking lot of the museum.

They made their way into the austere yellowed entrance of the building, down the empty corridors and to the lab she had shown him and Kaden the day they had met. Though he was in the same place he had been, everything was so different and such a disaster.

She flicked on the lights. The black table stood empty in the center. Walking over to the other side of the room, she dug around on the shelves that were covered with various bins, lights, and knickknacks. She pulled a dusty backpack out and slapped it against her leg.

"Here," she said as she handed it to Beau.

"Thanks." He opened the bag. A trowel and a few tools were inside.

The shrill beep of Ariadne's phone pierced the tense air. Ariadne pulled the phone from her purse and frowned. Her finger hovered over the button to answer.

"Who is it?" Trina asked.

"Kat texted." Ariadne looked up.

"And?" Beau growled.

She pushed the button and read the message out loud. "Talked to the priest. Stop what you are doing. Or you will force my hand."

The priest must have overheard them talking.

"What does she mean?" Beau stepped to Ariadne's side and put his hands on her shoulders. "Are you in danger?"

Ariadne shoved the phone in her pocket. "I'm tired of her and her power plays. She can't hold me back any more. For once, I'm going to do what is right instead of being one of her little slaves."

There was a strange jerk in his chest. *Is it love?*

He looked into her beautiful golden eyes and the tightening in his chest grew more intense. Running his hands over her shoulders, he drew them to her neck and pulled her softly to his lips.

He shouldn't, but the heat of her lips melted away the hesitancy—he was in love. This woman in his hands was giving up everything she knew to help him and Kaden. No one had ever been more selfless or giving. The curse loomed over him, but he couldn't help the feelings that rose within him as their flesh touched.

His mouth wandered up toward her ear. *Should I tell her that I love her?*

As his lips brushed against her ear lobe, she jerked back.

"We need to hurry. If Kat's coming after us, we are going to need to get in and out." Ariadne turned her back to him and walked to the other side of the table.

Dumbfounded, he stood with his hands up, as if she would come back into them.

Maybe it is better this way, her not knowing the way I feel. There's no way she can feel the same way I do. She's only helping us out of guilt.

He dropped his hands to his sides as he tried to push aside his feelings. Ariadne was right; they needed to get out of there. Trina stepped next to him and patted his arm.

From behind the lab table, Ariadne turned to face him with a blank look on her face. She bent over, opened the cabinet under the table and disappeared. "Only nymphs have ever been down here."

There was a whir of machinery as they shifted the cupboard upwards. The floor trembled. He walked to Ariadne's side. "What's down there?" he asked, as he stared down at the growing black hole in the floor.

"The temple of Epione. My…" she looked over at Trina and smiled. "I mean our, Goddess' shrine."

Ariadne stepped down into the blackness and pushed another switch. Fluorescent lights flickered to light and illuminated a steep staircase. He and Trina followed her as she made her way downward.

He slung the backpack high on his shoulder and walked through a set of marble columns. The cold room had a circle of chairs inside and on the far wall was a painting of a stunning woman with a sacral knot between her breasts and snakes wrapped around her arms. She held a glass stick as she stood in a clear spring. Pale people were sitting around her, looking up. The picture was amazing and was done in the style of early Renaissance painters. Who had painted such an amazing and unknown piece? When he turned to the front of the room, his breath caught in his throat. "Wow."

"I know," Ariadne said, pointing at the massive golden statue. "Isn't she beautiful?"

Beau couldn't take his gaze off the golden idol that rose all the way to the ceiling. "Your goddess, Epione, is the snake goddess?"

The effects of just this revelation will be huge in the scientific world. So much history will have to be rewritten. No, I can't. I can't tell anyone anything that I see.

He looked away from the woman with the snakes wrapped around her arms and stared at Ariadne. She walked to the altar and kissed a small ceramic figurine of the snake goddess. "My goddess," she whispered.

Trina followed Ariadne's lead. Bending, she kissed the statue's feet. "My goddess."

Should I follow? Or would that be sacrilegious? Unsure, he walked to the altar and bowed.

Ariadne smiled and stepped beside him and faced the idol. "Thank you, my goddess, for letting us borrow your relics. May they be blessed by your presence and help us to win the battle."

"Here." Ariadne handed him a dagger.

He pulled it out of the leather sheath that covered its blade.

Ariadne sucked in a breath. "Don't touch the blade, it's poisoned. It will kill just about anything."

He pushed the blade back down into the leather and carefully stuck it under his belt. "Can't everything be killed?"

Ariadne and Trina looked knowingly at each other and smiled. "Beau, not everything in this world is like you. There are many creatures that aren't human. There are many beings that have no compassion and no desires beyond killing."

"What do you mean? How do you know?" Beau stared at the mysterious women that stood in front of him.

Ariadne grabbed a ball of golden wire from the altar and stuffed it in his backpack. "I've been alive for thousands of years. I have seen most of what this world has to offer. There is a reason I choose to live in the human world."

"You have a choice?" There was so much he didn't know.

"I could live in my other form, as some other nymphs do. The Mustangs are known to act that way, but then again they are horses, not snakes like Trina and I."

"Excuse me? You're a snake now? A seducing snake?" This was almost too much to believe.

"I know it's a lot, but just trust me. I am trying to help you. And after we're done helping Kaden, you never have to see me again. You'll never have to think about what lives outside of your happy human world."

I could never forget this place. Or her.

Ariadne pushed her hair behind her ear and blinked her golden eyes. *Does she want me to forget her? How can I?*

She handed Trina a green bottle of wine.

"What? Are we planning on getting drunk before we go into the Labyrinth?"

"I wish," Ariadne said with a laugh. "But we're going to need every advantage we can get. I don't know what we're going to find down there."

"Hopefully, we will just walk in and take what we need." He paused. "What exactly is in the Labyrinth?" He looked over the altar, where bottles, knives, bows, and strange-looking mirrors shone back at him. "Isn't there something in here that'll work to cure Kaden?"

"I'm sorry, Beau, but this is just a temple for the healer. The weapons we have are only those that have been offered to Epione."

Beau stepped back. "Your goddess is a healer? Why can't we just pray to her? If she's real, wouldn't she just heal Kaden?"

"No, Beau," Ariadne said softly. "We have to go after the staff. Epione cannot heal without it."

"Oh. Why isn't her staff here in the temple?" He felt like a pain in the ass, but there were so many questions that were running through his mind.

"When we were cursed, it was taken to the Labyrinth to keep it safe and out of the hands of those who would use it to hurt others." Ariadne bowed to the statue. "Thank you, my goddess."

"We need to go." She strode to the bottom of the steps. "Kaden is waiting."

*

Ariadne dabbed sweat from her forehead as she pushed her shovel deep into the soil. They had already gone at least five feet deep behind the limestone column she had pressed her body against before she had shifted the first night. The entrance couldn't be much further.

Beau's cell phone beeped and he pulled it from his pocket and stared at the screen.

"Is Kaden okay?" Ariadne stepped closer and put her hand on his arm.

He dropped the phone back in his pocket. "It's just Vickie, she texted. Said she needed to talk to me about the governor."

She dropped her hand.

"She can wait."

Can't he see what the girl so desperately wants?

Ariadne tried to push the thoughts from her mind. He had made love to her. He hadn't told her to expect anything from their lovemaking, but it was fair to assume he wasn't chasing other women. Wasn't it?

Trina shrugged. "I'm gonna go stand guard. With it still being daylight, we're going to need an eye out here."

"Thanks." Ariadne dipped her head in appreciation. It was nice having someone on their side they could trust.

Trina climbed up and out of the hole, and the dirt showered down in her wake.

Beau's a good man, she thought, downplaying her persistent insecurities. *He wouldn't go for a college student. Would he?*

Stop. I have to stop. I need to focus on the here and now. We need to get in and out and be safe, so we can get back to Kaden. He's what really matters.

"Beau, hand me the wine, please?" Ariadne asked.

He opened the backpack and handed her the green bottle. Pulling the half-extended cork from the bottle's neck, Ariadne took a drink. The wine tasted of oak and tannins and carried with it the sweetness that came with age.

"Here." Ariadne passed the bottle to Beau.

He took a gulp.

"Now pour it onto the ground." She pointed to the place they had been digging. "We need to sacrifice."

The red wine splattered on the ground and up onto her legs, where it looked like the splatter of blood. The bottle empty, Beau dropped it with a thump.

Ariadne grabbed her shovel and threw a heap of dirt backward. She pushed the blade back into the soil, this time missing rock. Retracting the shovel, the ground shifted and fell in clumps into a void, exposing blackness. The scent of dank, stale earth wafted toward her from the hole.

"I found it! Beau, Trina, I found it!" She dropped the shovel and pulled at the earth exposing more of the cave's entrance.

Beau turned and hurried to her side. "Holy shit." He dropped to his knees. "Holy shit…I never thought I'd see this. I mean, I hoped I'd see this, but holy shit."

Trina peered over the edge of the pit. "Yes! Can you see anything?"

Ariadne smiled up at her. "No, but hopefully the staff isn't too far in. Maybe we can get in and out, then back to Kaden."

When Ariadne looked back at Beau, he was smiling and the sun seemed to shine directly on him, lighting his face. Leaning to him, she kissed his sweat-dampened cheek. She couldn't explain it, but seeing him glowing beside her made her heart flutter in her chest. The smile on his face, she had done that. She had made him happier than she had ever seen any living man. He looked better than a god.

"In its day, this place was marvelous. You can't imagine." Ariadne motioned toward the columns that stood crumbled on either side of the tunnel. "If you continue your dig, you might get an idea, but there were frescoes and ivory sculptures of the Minotaur standing on each side of the entrance. My father, Minos, had them erected after Theseus killed my half-brother. Right after the rain, when the sun shone down on the wet ivory, it was breathtaking."

He took her hand and brought to his lips. The touch of his mouth against her skin made the world blur around her. "Are you telling me the myth is true? Are you the one with the golden thread?"

She blinked, trying to focus. *Hopefully he didn't realize what a fool I had been. Falling for Theseus, and then having him run from me as soon as he was safe. Beau doesn't need to know my hideous, pitiful past.*

She wanted to look away, but instead she forced herself to look upon him. "I am."

"Wow," he said breathlessly. "I knew you were amazing, but mythical was more than I had imagined. I'm a lucky son of a bitch."

She couldn't stop her smile. "So you don't think I'm an idiot for falling for horrible men?"

"Hmmm," he said playfully. "So you think I'm a horrible man?"

The warmth from her cheeks multiplied. "I…you…I think you're great," she stammered. *Did he really think that I have fallen? Have I fallen? No. I can't, the risk is too high. I can't do that to him. I can't expose him to the curse.*

He ran his dirty fingers over her cheek. "You're pretty great yourself. And I want you to know that I know this took a lot to bring me here. You had to turn your back on your friends. I want you to know that I appreciate it."

"You know you can't tell anyone about this, right?"

He dropped his hand from her cheek and looked at the hole, then back at her. "This could change so much for me. It could change my future, Kaden's future. I won't have to worry about losing my job in Texas or about funding. I could do excavations wherever and whenever I wanted. People would come to me for answers."

She dropped the shovel into her lap. "What are you saying?"

"Nothing. I just—"

"Beau, you can't tell anyone," she interjected. "If anyone knows about this place, everything will change. Nymphs will be exposed."

Did he really consider selling her out? Would he use her to get what he had always wanted? Was he going to be like every man from her past? *No, Beau…please, don't.*

"Let's just get the staff thing and get back to Kaden," he growled.

His evasive answer made her stomach clench. "You can't tell anyone. Promise me."

"Fine." He reached toward the hole and chipped away at the harsh rock around the entrance.

She was torn. Her hands were paralyzed by the deep-seated insecurities of her past. A mixture of emotions, fear, anger, happiness, and apprehension all swirled inside of her. Could she really, truly trust Beau?

It was too late to turn back now. Kaden was depending on them.

Grabbing the shovel from her lap, she moved beside Beau and tamped away at the rocky soil. She had committed to this decision when she had gone against Kat's orders. Whatever would come her way, she had brought this upon herself and she would pay the consequences, but Kaden was far too wonderful of a boy to let him die. If Kat decided to murder her for her choice to save Kaden, at least Ariadne was going to do what she knew in her heart to be right.

It was possible she would give her life for Beau and his son, but instead of fear, she was filled with a sense of peace.

She prayed that Beau would eventually realize that each important moment in life required sacrifice. Hopefully, he would prove to be the man she hoped him to be, and understand that he needed to hide what she was showing him—even if it cost him his job and his reputation. His son's life was worth the price. For now, she would believe in him. And more importantly, she would believe and trust in herself.

Chapter Nineteen

They pounded away at the dirt until they were both out of breath, but the hole was big enough for them to fit through. "Trina?" Ariadne called.

"What's up?" Trina asked, as she peered over the edge of the dig.

"You stay up there. Don't let anyone down here or into the Labyrinth. I don't care who it is or what they say. Don't let them near this place. Do you understand?"

Trina nodded.

Ariadne turned to Beau. "Do you have the supplies?"

He patted the backpack at his side and gave her a curt nod.

"Hand me the wire."

He looked at her like she was making a sick joke. "Do you think that's really necessary? We aren't in the dark ages. We have GPS on our phone."

"Are you going to risk your life on the hope that your phone will work when we are deep underground?"

He tapped the phone that was stuffed in his back pocket as her words sank in. Reaching in the bag, he grabbed the ball of wire and tossed it to her. Taking an end, she tied it to the bottom of the limestone column that stood beside them. She stuffed the ball into her back pocket, so the thin wire would automatically feed out as they made their way through the maze of tunnels.

She stood up and leaned her shovel against the dirt wall. "Okay. I'll go in first and you can follow."

He stood up and he dusted off his pants. Grabbing his shovel, he leaned it next to hers against the wall. He turned to her, grabbed her arms and stared into her eyes. "I'm sorry, I shouldn't be angry.

I appreciate this. I hope you know that." There was softness in his round brown eyes.

"I know. And I hope you know…I trust you."

He let go of her arm and ran his hands over her hair. Putting his hand to the back of her head, he pulled her into his embrace. His lips crushed against hers as he held her tightly against his hot, sweaty body.

Releasing her from his hold, he looked down. "I want you to be careful. Don't do anything foolish."

"In case I haven't told you, there's only one thing that can kill me. So *you* don't do anything foolish."

He smiled and kissed her lips with a tenderness that reminded her of the night they had spent in the surf.

She pulled back, and then stopped and gave him one last quick peck on the lips. "Let's go."

Turning away, she faced the dark hole in the side of the wall. A new fear rose within her. The last time she had been in that place was with Theseus, and she had been badly wounded when a Chimera had attacked her and burned her with its fiery breath. Theseus had disposed of the creature, but the gods only know what atrocities he had left behind.

The rocks in the entrance scratched at her skin as she shimmied her way through the small opening. She sat up and jumped the last few feet to the floor of the tunnel.

The stagnant air of the Labyrinth was filled with the scents of burnt charcoal, rotting vegetation and decay. It had been over three thousand years since she had been here, but the scent was the same as it had been the first time. Bile rose in her throat, but she swallowed it away. *No weakness.*

Rocks tumbled from the entrance as Beau struggled to fit through the hole behind her. "You need help?" She turned to him in the darkness and extended her hand.

"No, ugh. I got this," he grunted.

Stubborn men…they'll never change.

She blinked as she let her eyes adjust to the blackness.

Beau jumped down from the hole and landed beside her. "Okay, which way?"

There were some things that had been lost from her memory forever, but not the day she had last experienced this place. "Left. At least that's the way Theseus and I went. But I can't say for sure where Kat put the staff."

"Well, left's as good a place as any to start looking." Beau took her hand and led her away from the security of the entrance.

She tried to control her fear of the dark tight walls that circled around her. Closing her eyes, she swallowed her fear. This was the time to be brave, to push past her comfort level. This was her time.

The further they moved away from the small hole, the darker it became until finally Beau clicked on his small LED flashlight. He flashed its beam at a wall and bugs scuttled frantically out of the brightness.

"Is it going to be like that the whole way?" He asked, pointing at where the bugs had been.

"When we get deeper, they'll lessen."

Their footsteps echoed in the eerie silence of the tunnels. Blindly, they moved forward until the tunnel came to an end. Beau shone the light down the right and the light was swallowed by the maw of blackness. To the left, the light hit the dull dry brown of a far wall, another T-shaped turn.

"Where now?" Beau asked as he flipped the light between their choices.

She pulled him to the right and moved into the endless darkness. The sounds of drips echoed up from the cavernous expanses as they zigzagged around corners. They followed a hairpin turn downward and it led them to a steep decline. The scraping of their shoes stopped and Beau flashed the light down, exposing a smooth-looking rock surface.

"Water must have seeped through cracks somewhere and deposited the minerals here." Beau pulled her closer as he spoke. "Be careful, sometimes these types of deposits can be slippery."

She smiled at his protective tone. "I'll be fine. From here on out, as far as I know, the floor will be like this."

"Do you think we should go toward the center?"

"Well, Kat obviously didn't lay the staff within the entrance like we were hoping. In the center of the maze, where Theseus killed the Minotaur, there is an altar of sorts. She might have put it there."

"Let's try it. Can you find the way?"

"That's where we're headed. As long as we continue down this way, I think we should be close. But when—"

A woman-like scream pierced through the still air.

Ariadne gasped. Beau clenched her hand. "That sounded like a cougar. You don't have cougars in Crete, do you?"

"We're not really in Crete anymore," she whispered. "We're in another world."

"What was that noise?"

"We don't want to see the being that made that noise." They came to a three-way fork. She peered down to the right, the known path, and then motioned for them to take the central corridor and away from the direction of the scream.

"What's it from?" Beau relaxed his grip.

"It's a spirit of death. If we meet her, you might not leave this place alive."

"So there's a banshee that lives here?"

"Worse than a banshee. The young woman, Fantasma, whose spirit roams this cave system, died not long after my adventures here. It was said that she fell in love with a mariner's son and she came from a wealthy Minoan family. When her parents found out about her love affair with the boy, they had him killed and told her that they had thrown his body into the Labyrinth."

Their footsteps echoed through the caves.

"What happened to her?" Beau whispered.

"Overcome with grief, she committed suicide and her spirit found the buried cave. Of course, her parents had lied and the girl never found her lover's body. Her wails are her anguished cries for her lover. When she meets anyone, she takes their body as an offering for the Labyrinth to release her love back to her."

Beau squeezed her hand tight. "There's so much that the world doesn't know that you do. I could add so much to the history books."

Her heart lurched. *Did he only care about science? Or was it his image he was so worried about?*

She thought for a moment. "In the past, history was written by politicians, without concern for the truth. Even with the change in technology, there is still a long way to go before the world and people are ready to learn the truth of their existence—and where they really stand in the greater order of life."

"Where is that exactly?"

"Somewhere right above dogs, but pretty low." Ariadne flinched as she spoke. "To most non-humans, they see you as a constant flow of chatter, an endlessly replenishing supply of workers, almost like ants. To most, you all look alike, without individuality."

"Do you think I'm an ant?"

She stopped and looked up into his eyes. There was sadness within them. "It would be easier if I wasn't close to your kind. I could think as they do, and I'd sit idly by and watch the short lives of humans play out below me. But I think humans can teach gods."

Beau frowned. "What can we possibly teach immortals?"

"Kindness, real love, sacrifice, and above all, humanity. Gods and all immortals lose a sense of themselves the longer they're alive. Things that were once important fall to the wayside. The fire of love is tempered by time. They become complacent and forget the feelings that once brought them joy. They forget what love is."

"Does that happen to your kind, to nymphs?"

She ran her thumb over the back of his hand. "Nymphs can't love, remember?"

His eyes were filled with the shadows of his insecurities. "Can't or won't?"

She picked up his hand and pressed it against her heart. "Can you feel it?"

His fingers uncurled from hers and pressed against her chest. For a moment, he let his hand rest above her left breast.

"My heart is just like yours. I feel the same feelings that you do. But I have to follow my mind as well as my heart. I can't expose others I care about to the curse."

"There are others?" Beau sounded hurt. "I thought I was the only one in your life."

The keen of the woman's scream echoed down the tunnels, and the sound seemed closer. "Shhh," she whispered. "Let's not forget why we're here."

He looked at her as if she were guilty of a thousand sins. "You're not getting out of this that easily. You will answer me, eventually."

She turned her back on him and led the way further down into the bowels of the earth. Love was off the table as far as she was concerned. In its place were the dangers that surrounded them. There were too many unknowns, and not just within the Labyrinth. She could never love a mortal man—unless she could find a way around the curse.

The drip of water echoed closer as they descended deeper, and the walls cried with their earthly tears. Beau stumbled behind her; his light flickered back and forth in the darkness, and cast a shadow in her path.

"You think we're close?" Beau said, breaking the tense silence between them.

"The Labyrinth, as far as I know, has another exit somewhere close to the palace of Knossos. But getting there—" Her foot slipped and her scream penetrated the darkness.

"Ariadne!" Beau yelled.

She reached out toward the walls, but her body continued to fall deeper, unstoppable as the flesh from her fingertips ripped away on the unforgiving cave walls. The wind whistled by her as she floundered.

Her feet hit first. The pain radiated up from the balls of her feet, into her ankles, all the way to her hips. She cried out as her body dropped and her head bounced off the wall. Sickening pain spread through her body and her mind went black.

Chapter Twenty

Beau shined his flashlight into the swirling blackness at his feet. "Ariadne?"

His heart thrashed in his chest. *God, please let her be okay. She can't be hurt…she just can't be…but the fall was so far. God, let her be alive.*

The golden wire from her pocket stretched tight over the harsh rock to his right. He tried to quiet the drumming of his heart, to listen if he could hear her from the depths. He held his breath. There was no sound.

"Ariadne?" He called again.

Nothing.

How am I going to get down?

Placing his hand against the rough volcanic rock wall, the water dripped down his hand and fell freely from his wrist. If he took his time he could work his way down, but he would need to be careful.

He opened his backpack and pulled out a rope. He looped one end around a small outcrop of rock on the side of the wall. Wrapping the other end of the rope around his waist, he fished the rope into an intricate knot.

He took another look down into the black depths. "Ariadne?" He silently pleaded for her to answer, but the only answer came in a chill that ran down his spine.

The flashlight trembled as he pushed the thin cord over his wrist. He would need both hands. Stepping to the edge of the precipice, he turned around and grabbed the rope.

He leaned backward as he shuffled down the side of the hole. His shoes slipped slightly, but he held firm and forced himself to take another step. His hands ached as each fiber of the rope dug into his hands, but he refused to let the pain register—Ariadne needed him.

Just when he began to wonder if the hole would ever end, his feet touched down. Unlooping the rope from his waist, he stuffed it in his bag. His numb hands fumbled with the cold metal flashlight. On the ground next to where he stood, Ariadne laid in a crushed heap. Her hair was thrown over her face, and her arm was contorted in a sickening V-shape.

A gasp escaped him.

Hadn't she said nymphs couldn't die?

He put his fingers to her neck. There was a faint pulse.

"Sweetheart?" he said, as he pushed back her hair, exposing her face.

Her eyes were closed and a torrent of blood streamed from her nose. He brushed the rest of her hair out of her face, but she didn't respond.

He looked up toward the heavens. "Please, whatever gods are out there. Please, help her. She needs you. Damn it, I need you. Come on."

What was he going to do? He couldn't jar her by carrying her around the tunnels. What if she had a spinal injury?

Closing his eyes, he ran his fingers over her cheeks. Her skin was cold. He had to do something. He needed to get the staff.

Beau leaned over her body, and gingerly took the ball of golden wire from her back pocket. He pushed it into his jeans pocket.

He cradled her neck and carefully rolled her crumbled body onto her back. Taking off his jacket, he draped it over her body. Taking the edge of the jacket's sleeve, he dabbed the blood away from under her nose. Leaning in, he softly kissed the pale skin of her cheek.

"Ariadne, sweetheart, I'll be right back. Trust me." She couldn't hear him, he was sure, but the action made him feel better.

Somewhere deep inside her mind, she would know that he was going after help in an attempt to make things right.

Standing up, he picked up his backpack and looked at Ariadne's face. A bruise was beginning to form under her eyes and her nose looked crooked. She was going to be sore when she woke up, but at least she was alive.

His footsteps echoed the beat of his heart. He turned back toward Ariadne and flashed the light in her direction, but the beam was quickly swallowed by the dank tunnel.

He turned back and continued walking. Nothing could approach her. He blocked the entrance. If anything wanted to find her it would either have to fall down the hole, or get through him.

The spool of gold wire unwound from his back pocket as he made his way down the straight corridor. Ten paces, twenty, thirty, forty. Somewhere around one hundred sixty paces he lost count. Stopping, he looked back, but there was only the inky world behind him.

"Ariadne?"

No answer.

He walked another fifty paces and came to a ninety-degree turn. No other paths had intersected into this one, at least that he had seen. They were in the clear.

For a second he felt like Dorothy from the *Wizard of Oz*. *There's no place like home. There's no place like home.* But no amount of clicking his heels was going to get him out of the hell he had created for himself, his son, and Ariadne. And he had created this hell when he'd been after glory and one-upping his colleagues by going after the Labyrinth.

What would glory bring him that he didn't already have? He already had a great son, a great life, and his job…well, his credibility was shit at the university, but what did that matter? Those bastards could go to hell. The people that really mattered were more important than the judgments of some pretentious assholes.

Besides, even if he never told anyone else about this place, he would know that he had been right. He had found a place that everyone had thought fictitious. He had followed his desires for fame, recognition, and grandeur and it had brought him only heartache, a divorce, questionable colleagues, and now his son was sick—all because he had put his yearning for prestige before his family. Never again would he be such a fool.

When he turned the corner, a blue circle of light shone from the darkness. He stopped and stared.

Something didn't seem right. Ariadne hadn't mentioned anything about the staff glowing, but then again she hadn't mentioned much about the staff. There was nowhere to go but forward—to save his son and the woman he loved. He put his fingers to the knife at his waist. For a moment he wished he were back in Texas, where instead of a knife, there would've been a gun on his hip.

He shuffled his feet in the direction of the glowing light. He thought to the picture he had seen of the monstrous angler fish, which lived deep in the ocean and used its light to lure naïve little fish into its gullet. *Goddamn it, I hope I'm not the stupid little fish.*

He exhaled as he tried to calm his nerves. The hilt of the dagger was wet with his sweat.

The light which had he had first seen at about the size of a baseball grew to almost three feet wide as he moved closer. *Too big to be an angler fish.*

He squinted as he tried to make sense of the light as it seemed to vibrate.

"Hello?" He called.

A soft wind blew against his face. He pulled the dagger out and pointed it at the strange orb. "Who the hell's there?"

Please, no one answer.

A faint chill prickled up his spine. He forced his body to move forward.

The tunnel that surrounded him came to an end, and opened up into a wide room. The blue light was so bright that he flipped off his flash light and pushed it into his back pocket. He could clearly see the black walls around him.

The glow slowly began to dim and at the core of the orb, he could make out the shape of a woman. The light shone through her skin, her hair was as black as the wet walls of the cave that surrounded them, and her gaze was focused on him.

He stared at the woman's long white dress. The cloth flowed around her as if it floated on her skin. On her arms, there were the same black tattooed snakes that were on Ariadne's, except on this woman, they circled around each arm and curled and writhed like they were alive.

Under the glowing woman's feet was the golden head of a bull.

He stepped back into the shadowy tunnel.

"Stop." The woman's voice echoed.

What was he to do? Should he run?

"Beau?" The woman's voice was softer.

"Who are you?" he asked, trying to sound more courageous than he felt.

She smiled and motioned for him to step closer. "It's all right, Beau. I vow I haven't come to this world to hurt you."

He stepped out of the shadows and toward the beautiful woman who beckoned him. "That's a good man." She smiled at him like a mother to a child. "Do you love her?"

He felt a strange energy wash over him. His heart lightened in his chest and his fears disappeared.

The beautiful woman smiled. "I have seen you with Ariadne. I've seen the hunger in your eyes and the need in your touch. Do you love her?"

"I...I love her," he stammered.

The glowing woman stepped down from the bull's head. "Do you know of the curse?"

He nodded. "Who are you? Are you going to kill me because I love her?"

"So you do know of the curse." She laughed, but the sound wasn't dangerous, instead it was pitying and the wave of calm washed over him again. "I'm not here to hurt you. I believe in true love and the power that it exudes. What you and Ariadne have is special."

Beau shook his head. "She doesn't know how I feel."

"She may not be ready to accept it, but she knows. Every woman knows when a man is in love. And you would have never forgiven her for what she had done to your site if you didn't love her."

Is the woman right? Had I loved her even then?

"Who are you?"

"I'm Epione, the goddess of all Nymphs. You should know me; you came to my temple."

He thought back to the elaborate paintings on the wall, in which the sick sat around Epione's feet, waiting to be healed. "Epione, uhh, ma'am, I need your help. My son and Ariadne are hurt. I need you to help heal them."

"I must have my staff in order to heal a human."

"Do you know where it is? Ariadne said Kat hid it in here, but we haven't been able to find it."

"Katarina Homeros isn't all that she portrays herself as being. When she ran from my villa, I had instructed her to put the staff in the Labyrinth—to hide it away. But as she was running, she fell and the staff was shattered. In an attempt to cover up what she had done she buried the pieces around the island, so that no one could put them together again."

"Is that why she is so afraid of someone going to look for it? So no one finds out that she is a fraud?"

The goddess nodded solemnly. "Exactly. You're a smart man."

What was he going to do? If the staff were broken, the last hope he had in saving his son's life was gone. His stomach fell and nausea washed over him.

"Don't worry, Beau. We can still save your son," Epione said, with a soothing touch to his shoulder. "From the heavens, I watched where she placed the pieces. And one by one, I found them and put them together, mending the staff as best I could. The staff is almost complete."

"So you have it?" Beau was filled with a sudden surge of hope.

"I couldn't take it to the heavens with me, out of fear of Zeus' retaliation. So I decided to hide it here in the Labyrinth. Unfortunately, it's no longer where I left it, but I think I know where it is."

Epione stepped down and held out her hands to him. "Put away your dagger and take my hand. I will show you."

He looked down at the forgotten golden hilted dagger in his hand. Gently, he pushed it down into the sheath at his waist. Epione's glowing hand was still as he stared at the perfect skin of her palm.

"What about Ariadne? Why don't we go back to her?"

"And then what? Are you going to carry her?" Epione's voice carried a strange edge.

"If that's what I need to do. I will carry her to the ends of the earth. I made a mistake leaving her back there. I won't go any further without her."

Epione smiled, as if he had passed some test. "Let's go to her."

They followed the golden wire back to where Ariadne lay. Her nose was more swollen than when he had left, and the blue light of the goddess accentuated the bruising beneath her closed eyes.

He knelt down to her side. "I'm going to wrap her neck with my coat. Maybe it'll help stabilize her spine, but there's nothing I can do for her arm," he said as he motioned to her broken left arm. "Can you hold her neck still while I carry her?"

Epione gazed down at Ariadne. "I believe I can do something to help her. Once I could help others with just my touch, but I have been without the power of my staff since the day Zeus forced the curse upon us. Perhaps, however, since she is Nymph…"

Her flowing white dress splayed around her as she knelt down next to Ariadne's head. She rubbed her hands together and placed them gently on Ariadne's temples. Epione whispered in a strange high-pitched language. Closing her eyes, the goddess rubbed her fingers in slow circles. The glow of her skin brightened.

Her brows furrowed, a strange desperation came to her eyes, and her hands moved quicker. Her anxiety was contagious and his hands began to sweat.

The goddess has to fix her.

Beau lifted Ariadne's hand to his face and put her palm against his skin. She felt like ice. "Aria? Please. We need your help. Please, wake up."

He brought her fingers to his lips and brushed her skin against his. Epione's light again grew brighter.

"Don't stop, Beau," she ordered. She started another chant in her strange tongue.

Ariadne's nose straightened and her contorted arm pulled back into a normal shape with a subtle pop. The blood that had dried on her face began to disappear and the cuts beneath slowly faded into her skin. A faint pop like that of her arm setting came from her right leg.

He feathered his lips over Ariadne's soft fingers. up her index finger, over the tip, and down to the inside of her palm. His lips stopped at the head of the black snake in her palm. He could feel a strange quiver beneath his touch. Leaning back, he watched as her fingers slowly curled over the blinking snake.

"Ariadne?" He laced his fingers between hers and pulled them to his mouth. "Sweetheart?" He kissed her hand again.

Her eyes fluttered open. She stared at him, then glanced to the glowing goddess. "Beau? Epione?"

Epione stopped rubbing Ariadne's temples. "Yes? We are here, my sister."

Beau's heart pounded. He wanted to pick her up and pull her into his arms, but the fear of hurting her stopped him.

A thought struck him. "Epione, you healed Ariadne, do you think you could heal my son? We wouldn't need the staff…"

Epione looked at him with an expression of sadness upon her face. "She is different. She is Nymph, flesh of my flesh. I healed her as I would heal myself. Your son is human. It's an entirely different kind of magic."

He dropped his gaze from the goddess.

"I'm so sorry," Epione said. "But we will try to get the staff, I promise you."

Ariadne groaned.

"Are you okay?" Beau asked. "Do you hurt anywhere?"

With a slight groan, he helped her sit up. She rolled her neck and flexed her feet, inspecting her body. "What happened? All I remember is walking through the tunnels."

"It's my fault. I should've walked in front of you," Beau started. "You fell down a hole. I'm so sorry."

She looked at their entangled fingers and smiled. "It's not your fault." She glanced to Epione. "My goddess, I'm glad to see you, but how did you come to us?"

"Your lover…," Epione motioned to Beau. "He prayed for help when he found your body. I'm not sure if you are aware of it, but I have a soft heart when it comes to true love."

He stared at the goddess.

Did she say true love? She had to have been confused. Yes, he loved Ariadne. But true love meant that they both had to feel something, didn't it?

He looked back at Ariadne. She was looking at the ground at her feet.

Questions flew through his mind, but he couldn't bring himself to ask them. If she loved him, she would tell him. Damned sure, she wouldn't be staring at her feet.

Beau dropped her hand and stood up. "We need to get going." The backpack thumped as he threw it onto his back.

The goddess looked up at him with a knowing smirk. As he watched her, her glowing blue skin began to dim. She lifted her skirt and moved to stand up. He extended his hand and she accepted with a gracious tilt of the head. "It's a strange thing, life. One must look past their own judgments and insecurities in order to truly understand and love another."

Ariadne rolled to her knees.

Beau's heart clenched in his chest as he noticed a line of blood as it ran from her hair and down the skin of her pale neck. He let go of the goddess' warm hand, put his hands beneath Ariadne's arms and helped lift her to her feet. She grabbed his arm as she wavered.

"Are you okay?" he asked, with his hands still around her.

"I'll be fine." Ariadne moved out of his hands.

True love, my ass.

His hands dropped to his sides.

"My goddess, do you know where we can find the crystal staff Kat took from you?" Ariadne asked, as if she was unaware of the injury she had inflicted upon him.

"As a matter of fact I do, but I will be of no use in getting it. It is in a place no goddess or demi-god can reach."

"What? What do you mean?" Ariadne stammered.

"The staff is in the hands of the dead. And only Beau can retrieve it."

Chapter Twenty-One

The blue light of Epione's skin reflected off the black oil pool at their feet and made a macabre arc of rainbow colors on the walls around them. Ariadne's body ached and her head spun.

"What do you mean…we can't reach the staff?" she stammered. "We can't die. I can go after it."

"No," Epione said with a wave of her hand. "If we go in, we can't return to this world or the heavens. We would be condemned to spend the rest of eternity with Hades—as his private concubines."

Beau stepped close to her and took her hand. "What do you want me to do?"

The goddess pointed out at the slick. "The crystal staff is at the bottom of this pool, but this is no ordinary pool. When Ariadne's brother, the Minotaur, was killed, Poseidon was in a rage and in his anger caused the blood of the demi-god to flow untamed. The blood filled the tunnels of the Labyrinth, until Poseidon gained vengeance upon Theseus. This is what is left of that flood. It is said that this is a portal between this world and the afterlife. Spirits are free to come and go as they please, but if a living person touches the fluid they are forced to become a spirit of the underworld."

"After you fixed the staff, how did it get here?" Ariadne asked.

"Fantasma, the ghost, brought it to this place. She was looking for the spirit of her lover, hoping to bring him back from the dead with the staff, but he never surfaced. Eventually she grew distraught, and threw the staff into the lake."

Beau leaned over the edge. Ariadne grabbed him from behind and pulled him back. "What do you think you are doing?"

Beau frowned as if she had been wrong in stopping him from falling. "I was just looking to see if I could see it."

"What would have happened if you fell in?" Ariadne let go of the waist of his jeans.

"I wasn't even close," he said. "Don't worry."

There was no way she was going to let him risk his life for the staff. There had to be another way to heal Kaden. Maybe if she got Tammy even more—better—supplies, the witch could figure out a cure for the disease. Tuberculosis was a human disease, there had to be a cure—even if the illness had been brought upon by the Nymph's curse.

Epione stepped between them. "Beau, the staff is in the middle of the lake."

Beau lifted the hem of his shirt as he moved to strip it off.

"No," Ariadne interrupted. "Beau can't be put in any more danger. This is unacceptable."

"Ariadne is right. You mustn't touch the blood of the lake; if you do, you will become a spirit of the afterlife. We must come up with another way of finding the staff. Do you have anything in your bag that may prove to be useful?"

Beau dropped the bag from his shoulder and pulled the zipper open. Shuffling around the contents, he brought out a dirty rope. "I used this to climb down the hole, it should hold up." He handed it up to Ariadne and then went back to the rest of the contents of his bag.

Ariadne tried to peek inside. "You don't have a grappling hook in there, do you?"

"No, but I do have a trowel. Maybe if we bent it, it could act like one." He pulled the worn, slightly rust-speckled trowel out from the bag.

The way he bit his lip as he thought, made Ariadne's pulse rise. He was so sexy. Beau let go of his lip, stood up, stepped over to the wall and picked up a rock. A loud twang of rock against metal pounded through the cave, forcing her to cover her ears from the vibrating sound. Whatever was down there with them would be called into the sound—they wouldn't have much time.

The sound stopped and he held up the bent hook-like piece of metal. "This should work. It'll be just like fishing."

Except there is more than one life on the line.

"I know you love Beau." Epione leaned into Ariadne's ear and whispered. "And perhaps it doesn't have to mean a death sentence…"

"What?" Ariadne said her voice filled with shock.

Epione nodded.

Did her goddess have a way around the curse? If there was a way, it could change everything. It could change everything for her and her kind. For once, they would have real freedom.

"How?" Eagerness filled her voice.

"We must get the staff first and heal Kaden, and then I will share my secret with you. Until then, we need to keep Beau safe," Epione whispered with a gentle smile.

"Please—"

"I think I got it," Beau said as he held up the bent trowel.

Ariadne blinked. *I can love him…*

"Are you okay?" Beau asked.

"She's fine." Epione rubbed Ariadne's arm, but Ariadne was numb.

They needed to get out of this place.

Beau frowned, but set back to work. He reached into the bag and took out a pair of latex gloves. He pulled them onto his hands. "See, Ariadne. I've got this under control…don't panic."

His words only made the sinking feeling inside of her deepen.

Beau tied one end of the line through the hole in the handle of the mangled trowel and the other end, he tucked under his foot. With a heave, he thrust the makeshift hook out into the blood lake. The object hit the liquid with a sickening splash. He let the hook settle. Slowly he pulled the blood-covered rope backward until the hook rested on the bank.

He threw it out again. Ariadne held her breath as he pulled. It came to a stop and he tugged.

"Did you hit something?" Epione asked.

"I think so," he answered over his shoulder.

Praise the goddess.

Hand over hand he brought the rope in. A glass ball broke through the inky surface about five feet from where they stood.

"I think I got it," Beau exclaimed.

The glass ball dropped down out of sight.

"What?" Beau shouted as the rope jerked in his hands. "Something is pulling!"

"The dead must not be ready to give up their prized possession." Epione moved next to Beau and lifted her hands over the pond. "Ariadne, come help me, together our power is stronger."

The thought of helping her goddess made her nervous. Seduction had been her only skill, and it was marginal at best, but she stepped next to the goddess and lifted her hands in imitation.

"Spirits of the underworld, we come to you with open hearts," Epione said in the old tongue. "I wish to take back the staff that once belonged to me. People are in need of me, to help stall their delivery to the underworld. With my beloved staff, perhaps I can help your brothers, sisters, sons, daughters, grandchildren and friends."

Beau watched as if they were telling secrets that he wasn't privy to.

Epione began an old song to the dead, a song Ariadne had long forgotten. "*We remember you upon the earth, fresh and strong like an olive tree, bearing fruit and bringing joy, until death broke your earthly chains. You fell as ash upon the earth, covering it with your spirit. From the ash, new life has formed and continues in your memory, carrying your essence. You will never be forgotten.*"

Epione balled her fists and raised them to the sky. "Come into the light and speak to me. Then I pray you go in peace and dance as a child upon the wind."

The melody brought chills to her skin.

A black skeletal hand emerged from the blood. Behind it raised a gaunt blackened head, with no hair, sunken eyes and mummy-like thin lips. The being opened its mouth and a flurry of bugs flew out from the opened maw.

Ariadne grabbed Beau's arm and forced him to stand behind her, away from the grotesque creature as the scent of death wafted toward them.

"I have only one thing left in this world. You may not take the staff," the skeletal woman said as her cold voice echoed off the blood lake.

Epione looked at the being without even a flicker of disgust. "I understand completely, Fantasma. Have you found the mariner's son, the boy you once loved?"

The long-dead woman barely shook her head.

"I'm so sorry, my child," Epione said. "If we helped you, would you be willing to give us the staff?"

The woman remained still for a moment, then in a stiff motion, nodded.

"What was the boy's name?" Epione asked.

The woman quivered. "Gino."

Epione began chanting again, singing the same song, this time calling to Gino. A large black hand broke to the surface, followed by the sunken face of whom Ariadne assumed to be Gino.

The sunken woman peered to her right as the man turned to face her. "My love," he said, in a voice as aged and dry as the skin across his bony chest.

"Why haven't you come to me?" Fantasma choked, her voice filled with long-buried emotion.

Gino pulled his hand out of the lake and in it was the staff.

Ariadne gasped as droplets of the inky blood ran down along the lines of the cracked surface. The top of the staff was a carved snakehead with what appeared to be ruby eyes. Below the eerie head, two wings extended outward, like a flying bird. Looking closer, she could see the body of the rod was a snake and around it, two snakes were entwined in a perfect swiveling pattern.

The ghastly man stared at the skeletal woman. "My love, I have always been with you. Why would you think you were alone?"

"I've been searching…"

"When I left this world I left it knowing that I loved you. I had been granted a gift few have had the honor of receiving. Even if brief, I had true love in my life. I had no reason to stay behind."

The skeletal woman fell into Gino's arms. "I love you. I have always loved you. We can be together forever. Take me home, Gino, my love."

Gino pushed the forgotten staff into Epione's waiting hands.

Kaden would be saved. But would Beau be good to his word and tell no one of this place?

Chapter Twenty-Two

The dim light of dusk streamed through the entrance and littered the floor in front of them. He pulled the last bit of golden wire around the spool and stuffed it into his backpack. They had been below too long and his body ached to get back to his son's side. The thread of life Kaden had left this morning was undoubtedly getting thinner each second.

He looked up as the light from the entrance shifted. Beau put out his hand and stopped Epione and Ariadne from going any further. Something was wrong.

He rushed toward the entrance and peered out. "Where the hell did Trina go?" He pointed toward the empty ledge.

Ariadne ran up to his side and looked out. "Maybe she got tired and sat down. Trina is my sister and she loves Kaden. She wouldn't let us or him down." There was a tense edge to her voice.

"Do you think Kat found us?" Beau looked over to Ariadne. There was fear in her eyes.

Before she could answer, a gray cat with a crooked tail and golden eyes stepped out from the darkness and wrapped itself around Beau's legs. Beau pulled the dagger from its sheath and pointed it at the unexpected beast.

"Really, Beau? You wish to kill a cat?" Epione said, as she squatted down and rubbed her fingers together, beckoning the cat toward them. "This is not a normal cat. Reveal yourself, witch."

The cat mewed with an annoyed flick of its ears. Looking up at him with its sparkling eyes, its body pulled and stretched. He blinked. There was so much he didn't know. Not only were there witches, there were shape-shifting witches as well. The world was becoming less familiar with each passing minute.

A naked gray-haired woman with ample bosoms stood before him where the cat had been only moments before. He recognized her from somewhere.

"Hey y'all," the woman said, extending her hand to Epione.

The goddess politely tipped her head, but kept her hands firmly clasped at her waist. Beau forced himself to step forward and shake the woman's hand.

Tammy smiled brightly at him. "We all haven't really been formally introduced, but I'm Tammy Blithe. I just came to warn y'all."

He pulled his hand from her gripping, cat-paw-like hands. "About what? Is Kaden okay?"

"Kaden's doing all right for now, he's a li'l better than this mornin'. I heard about him seeing the priest."

Beau bristled. Kat wouldn't go after his son, would she?

Ariadne moved toward the entrance and peered out. "What happened to Trina?"

"Kat had the other nymphs take her. I think she's fine, but Kat and Stavros have an ambush waiting outside." Tammy pointed out past the edge of the pit. "I heard them talking about a staff…I don't think they want you to be taking anything outta this place."

"Why Stavros? He doesn't have a dog in this fight? Does he?" Beau glanced over toward Ariadne.

Ariadne nibbled at her bottom lip. "Maybe Kat finally convinced him it wasn't a good idea to expose the Labyrinth and the staff. The staff is extremely powerful and in the wrong hands, it could prove to be disastrous. Something with its power could start a war."

"And a war isn't good for a country that's financially strapped," Beau said, finishing her sentence.

"Exactly." Ariadne nodded. "What do they have planned, Tammy?"

Tammy shrugged. "Well, there're a bunch of funny-looking men who stink to high heaven."

Epione sniffed the air. "Muroidea, I suspect."

"Ratters? You're probably right. We saw some the other day at the Mouse Hole," Ariadne said.

Tammy stepped to look out of the entrance. "They are waiting out in the parking lot for y'all. Didn't want you to be able to escape." She pointed down the caves.

Beau looked into the swallowing darkness. "Do you think we could find the other exit?"

The goddess closed her eyes and muttered magical words. After a second, she opened them. "It's quite a distance. It'll take us at least a few hours to get to the other side, and that's if we don't run into any more trouble."

"Let's go." Tammy walked down into the cave and waved for them to follow.

"No." Ariadne shook her head. "We're going to face them."

Tammy's gaze flickered to the entrance, then back to Ariadne. "That Kat's gotta hell of an axe to grind with you."

Ariadne rubbed her hands over her face and sighed and for the first time, Beau noticed how tired and drawn she looked. "I just want to help Kaden."

Beau stepped to her and squeezed her hand.

"Aria." Tammy sighed. "That's not how Kat sees it. She thinks you're trying to take her place at the head of y'all's sisterhood."

"I should've known she would think that. All she cares about is power and prestige. She needs to control." Ariadne shook her head.

"Let's go." Ariadne motioned to the hole in the wall. "We'll hope for the best, but be ready to fight. Watch me closely, I'll go out by myself and see if we can talk it out. If something goes wrong, come at them with everything you have."

Tammy licked her lips. "Stavros is mine."

Ariadne pointed at the witch. "You can't kill him."

"But he killed Ms. Angelica," Tammy said in a pout. "And that little Vickie failed."

"Vickie was the one who shot him?" Beau said, as a wave of shock passed over him. "But why?"

Tammy snickered. "She's real fond of ya, that one is. Didn't want to go home, I 'spect."

It all made sense. She had been the only person who hadn't been at the meeting with Stavros and she'd been obvious in her flirtation. Why hadn't he seen it before?

"Does Stavros know?" He shuddered at the thought of what the governor would do to the young girl if he found out that she had tried to assassinate him.

"I heard him talking to Kat about it," Tammy said.

"What's he going to do to her?" Beau couldn't help the feeling of fear that crept through him for the girl.

"It sounds like he's already caught her. She's still alive, but for how long, I dunno."

He barely liked his student, but the thought of the governor enacting martial law on the girl pissed him off. "Let's go. That bastard needs to be taken out."

Ariadne frowned. "Killing is for the wicked. There has to be another way to make him pay."

Beau started. "He deserves—"

"I'll figure out somethin', but it ain't gonna be pretty." Tammy interrupted. "There ain't no reason for ya to get your hands dirty, Beau. You're a good man."

There was a clatter of stones and they all stopped and stared out through the hole in the wall. No one was there, but Beau's heart raced. They needed to get moving.

"My goddess," Ariadne said with a bow of the head. "Is there a way that you can go to Kaden? We need him to be taken care of and you need to stay protected."

The goddess looked down the maze and nodded. "I'll meet you at the hospital."

Epione's iridescent blue body began to fade. Before Beau could take a shocked breath, she and the staff she had been holding disappeared.

"Let's go." Beau walked to the wall and stuffed the knife back in the sheath.

His muscles strained as he pulled his body out of the belly of the underworld. He extended his hand to help Ariadne to her feet as she stepped out of the darkness.

Tammy smiled and without a sound, shifted back into her gray cat form and jumped out of the hole. She looked back at them before she made her way to the edge of the pit, jumped up and out, and disappeared into the evening light.

There was a keen of laughter that echoed down to them from the parking lot.

Great. We can catch them unprepared. Beau smiled. He balled his hands into fists and the excitement surprised him. He hadn't been in a real fight in a long time.

Ariadne stood up. "Wait here," she ordered in a whisper.

Every cell in his body wanted to follow her, but he nodded.

She climbed up the edge of the pit and out into the night. The moonlight made her appear as a silhouette in the night as the crunch of her footsteps moved away from him.

"Hey, Kat. What're you doing here?" He heard Ariadne ask. "Who're your friends?"

His heart thrashed in his chest. It felt so wrong to hide away and let her face the dangerous situation without him.

He looked over the edge of the pit. Ariadne was standing next to Kat and Stavros, beside Stavros' black town car. A thickset man with beady eyes and a wide nose stood next to Governor Kakos, who kept glancing frantically around as if he wished for an escape. Kat must have convinced him that what she wanted was right. But now faced with the situation, the governor looked out of place as he pulled at his necktie and shifted his feet.

Across the parking lot to the left were the four men from the

Mouse Hole standing in a tight circle. A man with a black eye patch stared at Ariadne and then motioned to the other men in the group. They looked as if they were about to pounce.

He jumped over the edge of the pit and raced toward Ariadne, blade in hand.

The man with the wide nose smirked at him.

"Hey, doc." The man with the eye patch flashed a vicious smile.

Ariadne turned toward him, a frown on her face.

"Hey," he said, with a faked shortness of breath. He motioned to Ariadne. "Why didn't you wait for me? I thought I saw the staff back there."

Kat's eyes brightened. "You didn't find the staff?"

Ariadne flashed him a smile and then turned back to Kat. "No, I'm afraid not. You don't know where we could find it, do you?"

Kat looked at Stavros, and then at the group of men. Guilt flashed over her face. "I'm not going to tell you. You have no business being down there. And you had no business going against the sisterhood." Kat's hands pulled into tight fists.

"We found out about what you did, Kat...Epione came to us. You broke the staff and have been lying to cover up your mistake. Your lie will be exposed."

Ariadne smiled viciously. "The sisters will come to know you as a fraud."

Kat hissed. "From the moment you opened your smart little mouth, you guaranteed I would have a mutiny." Kat motioned toward the group of nasty-looking men. "And unlike you, I came prepared for a fight."

"I have no intention of telling the world about the Labyrinth or the staff," Ariadne said, her voice strong.

Kat glared. "I don't believe you, or your little boy toy."

Stavros backed up against the town car. "I never wanted things to go like this..."

"Shush, Stav," Kat said, as she brushed her fingertip seductively over the governor's lips.

Kat turned to the group of men and snapped her fingers. "Boys! Do your bidding!"

There was the crunch of feet on the gravel and Beau turned as the rats moved into an attack position around him.

"Son of a bitch," Beau muttered.

"Ah, he must remember his little 'asshole' comment," the wide-nosed man said with a dangerous laugh.

"Take care of him." Kat pointed at Beau.

The man with the wide nose began to shrink and the rest of the men across the lot followed his lead until there were only heaps of clothing left on the ground. Through the neck hole of the leader's shirt, a fat gray rat at least three times the size of a normal rat poked its head out. The oversized rat had a wide nose and red-rimmed eyes.

"What the hell?" Beau said to no one.

The beady eyes of the rats were trained on him and he readied himself for a fight.

Kat eyed Ariadne with a predatory glare. "You went against *me* and you took a human down into the Labyrinth. You exposed us all. You must pay."

"I have no desire for money or power," Ariadne countered. "This isn't about that. Is your ego really that sensitive that you can't just admit that you aren't who you have claimed to be?"

Kat hissed. "Shut up. You're not to be trusted."

"You lied to me…and to the sisterhood. They need to know who you really are. You've been pretending to be the savior of the staff from the very beginning. You have deceived all of us. You're the one who isn't to be trusted."

Kat's face reddened with anger.

"Aria, sweet—"

Before Stavros could finish whatever he had tried to say, Kat pounced and landed on top of Ariadne and grabbed her hair. "You had no right going into the Labyrinth!"

Ariadne thrashed beneath Kat's grip. With a ferocious kick, she flipped Kat on her back and clasped her throat.

Beau chased after her, the knife still in his hand. The squeal of rats pierced the air. "Stop, Ariadne!"

But she didn't look back as her fist raised and she brought it down upon Kat's wide-eyed face.

Before he could reach her, the women were entangled in a mess of fists. The thug stepped between the women and Beau, carefully avoiding the extended knife. "You need to let them handle this," he grumbled.

"Get out of my way." Beau tried to push past the stout man, to no avail.

Kat yelped as Ariadne landed another punch.

He turned as the squeal and scratching sound of the rats grew louder. There was a tug on the leg of his pants as the beady-eyed rat ascended upward. He kicked and tried to fling the rat, but instead the monster's teeth pierced through the fabric of his jeans and deep into the flesh of his shin. The beast shook Beau and its razor-like teeth shredded his skin.

Beau fell to the ground, his shoulder taking the brunt of his fall. He slammed the knife down. The blade sank deep. A blood-curdling squeal pierced the air. He plunged the blade in again and the squeal turned into a strange gurgle. The pressure released on his shin and the beast fell to the ground.

Before he could recover, the other giant rats were upon him. One tore at his arm, another at his already mangled leg. The third launched through the air, straight at his throat. He tried to roll, but the rat on his leg stopped him with its heavy cat-sized body.

Blindly he thrust the dagger upward, hoping it would find its mark. Ariadne's scream rattled the air as the dagger skewered the rat's underbelly. The rat squealed and struggled around the blade.

The rats on his leg and arm stopped as the skewered rat's eyes went dark. They released his flesh and darted into the shadows with a furious scratching noise.

He threw the dead rat off himself. A cat yowled and hissed and the scratch of the rat's nails stopped.

"Ariadne?" He forced his mutilated body to stand.

"Beau! Help me!" she cried, but the sound was muffled.

Across the parking lot, the thug, the governor, and Kat attempted to load her thrashing body into the trunk of Kat's car. Ariadne's legs flailed and whipped around as she struggled.

He ran as fast as his legs would allow.

Kat looked shocked and surprised as the governor dropped Ariadne's legs and ducked behind the other side of the town car.

The eye-patch-wearing thug turned as Beau's punch connected with the side of his temple. The man crumpled to the ground.

"Ariadne," Beau said between ragged breaths. "I'm here. Kat, drop her!"

There was the hiss and screech of a cat, and Stavros screamed.

Beau looked over just as Tammy, in her cat form, climbed up Stavros' body. Stavros tried to grab at the cat, but she held on and before he could get hold of her, she landed a vicious bite to his hand. Then another.

"Aggh!" Stavros screamed.

Tammy jumped down as Stavros sank to the ground. He tried to speak, but no sounds escaped him.

Tammy shifted out of her cat form and looked down at the man. "That's for Angelica. You're one lucky bastard Ariadne still cares about ya, she's the only reason you ain't dead." Tammy kicked the man. "And don't ya dare do nothing to that Vickie girl. Ya deserved what ya had coming to ya."

Stavros put his hands to his throat and he nodded. His head dropped to the ground and his eyes rolled back in his head, but Beau felt no pity.

"Get off of me!" Ariadne jerked out of Kat's hands.

"I didn't want to do this," Kat hissed. She reached into the open trunk and pulled out a shed snakeskin. "I was just hoping to talk some sense into you."

"You bitch!" Ariadne grabbed after the skin.

Kat stared at him. "Beau, did Ariadne ever tell you what happens when a shed is destroyed?" Her smile was dangerous. "It's almost like a voodoo doll. One little tear…" Kat pinched the skin with her fingers.

"Stop!" Ariadne yelled. "Don't you dare." Ariadne stood still and stared at the skin. "How did you get my shed?"

"I've been your leader for how long? And you think that I don't know you hide your sheds in the temple?"

"Give me the shed. Or I *will* kill you," Ariadne said in a deadly voice.

"You wouldn't dare." Kat attempted to stare her down, but Ariadne didn't waver.

"Beau, hand me the dagger." Ariadne didn't break her gaze, but opened her hand.

"Stop." He stepped in between the women, careful not to turn his back to either. "You are sisters. It doesn't have to be this way. Kat, give me the shed." He held out his hand.

"No," Kat growled.

He lifted the blade to her face. "If you don't give me the shed, I'll kill you myself."

"Didn't she tell you? You can't kill us." Kat snickered.

He lifted the blade higher and pushed it to her throat. "This is Tammy's poisoned dagger, from the temple, or weren't you aware?"

Kat's eyes widened. "You took him to the temple?"

Ariadne smiled. "I trust him."

"But…what? How could you?" Kat stammered.

"I'm done being held back by my past." Ariadne stepped toward Kat and pulled the shed skin from the woman's hand. "Now you can come help me move our kind into the future, or you can go hide away."

Ariadne carefully folded the skin and stuffed it into her pocket. "Frankly, I don't care what you do, but if you come with us I'll treat you better than you have treated me. To start with, I won't tell anyone about your little mishap with the staff."

"You won't?" Kat stared at her.

"I promise. Besides, Epione has repaired it."

Kat looked stunned.

"We are going to the hospital. If you attempt to stop us, I'll expose what you've done and all that you have done to hide the truth from us." Ariadne paused, as if to let her words sink in. "Now, do you wish to join us?"

Kat nodded faintly. "Are you taking over the sisterhood?"

"You can help lead the ceremonies, but there will be no defined leader. I want us to work together without the restraints of hierarchy," Ariadne said. "We are sisters, equal and united. We must learn to trust each other again."

Kat looked over to Beau.

Ariadne followed her gaze. "And you'll have to trust Beau. He'll keep his promises. I know it. Not all men are like Stavros and Theseus. Some men are good, they mean what they say."

Kat stepped back, away from the blade at her throat. "Fine. When he goes against us, it's your responsibility."

"Do I need to remind you that you'll no longer threaten me?"

Beau lifted the blade as an evil reminder of what was at stake.

"Fine. We're equal." Kat said begrudgingly.

"Can I trust you? Or does Beau need to take care of you?" Ariadne motioned to the knife in his raised hands.

Kat looked down at the silver blade, then up at him. "I won't stop you."

"Good." Ariadne turned to Beau.

She reached over to him, putting her hand to his arm. He

could feel the warmth of her skin against his and a strange calming energy flowed through her touch. "It's okay," she whispered.

Ariadne gently put her hands next to his on the dagger and pulled. His fingers uncurled from the hilt and let her slip the dagger from his grip.

"Kat, you need to take care of the rats. We don't need a crime scene at Dr. Morris' site." Ariadne looked over at him. "He needs to have time to fill it in."

It took a moment for her words to sink in. Could he fill in the site? Hide the Labyrinth? Act as if he'd never found this place? There was fear and questions in Aura's eyes. He gave a tiny nod. He had promised her he would tell no one.

Ariadne smiled and turned back to Kat. "When you go, take Stavros with you."

Tammy stepped out away from Stavros. "He should be up and running in a coupla days. When the poison from my claws runs out of his system, make sure he knows that he's never gonna mess with us witches again."

"You heard her, Kat." Ariadne nodded. "Tammy, you probably want to get out of Crete before he wakes up."

Tammy looked over at Beau and smiled. "Give Kaden a hug for me."

Beau smiled. "Will do, Tammy. Will do."

The witch slipped back into her cat form and sprinted off into the night.

Beau took hold of Ariadne's warm hand. "Let's go. I need to be at my son's side."

Chapter Twenty-Three

Epione leaned over the side of the white plastic rail of the hospital bed. The lights were off and the only glow came from the sun that peeked out from behind the closed curtains. Kaden's eyes were closed and his skin pale, but the machines pulsed and beeped in a comforting steady rhythm.

The door clicked shut behind Ariadne and Beau and the noise from the nurse's station grew muffled and distant.

"They won't come in, will they?" Ariadne motioned in the direction of the nurses outside of the room.

Epione looked up. "I put a charm on the door. No one else will be permitted to enter."

Epione put her hands on top of the crystal staff that sat on Kaden's chest and closed her eyes and muttered what Ariadne assumed to be a charm.

Beau crossed the room and made his way to the head of the bed. "How's he doing?"

Epione eased open her eyes and looked up to Beau. "He's responding slightly, but I think I'm going to need all of our strength." Epione motioned to her.

Ariadne stepped to the side of the bed beside Beau. She laid her hands upon Kaden's chest, over his heart. "Is this correct?"

Epione nodded. "Do you remember the old words?"

Ariadne thought back to the shaded memories of her past. "I think so."

Beau stroked the skin of Kaden's forehead as Epione placed her cool hands over Ariadne's.

Epione spoke in the old tongue and Ariadne followed. "*Gods above, we call to you. We pray that you aid us in the journey of healing. May our light fill the heart of those who seek healing, and mend all wounds.*"

The crystal staff began to glow with a pure white light.

Epione continued the prayer. "*Light of thy staff, shine into the lungs. Shine into his heart and brighten his pulse. Shine into his mind and freshen his thoughts.*"

The staff brightened as Epione hummed a song foreign to Ariadne.

Epione began to sweat and her brows furrowed as she concentrated upon the healing. "Kaden, let the light heal you."

Kaden's eyes trembled, as if he had tried to respond.

"That's good," Epione said her voice smooth and calming. Her song flittered throughout the room.

The machines in the room began to alarm. Ariadne looked up and watched as Kaden's heartbeat raced across the monitor. Beau had a worried look on his face, but didn't stop stroking his son's forehead. "It's all right, kiddo. It's okay," he reassured over and over again.

The racing lines of the heart monitor slowed.

Epione looked up at them with a smile. "I think we did it. He's going to be okay."

Ariadne's heart raced with excitement. Kaden would be okay.

"Kaden?" Beau ran his hand over his son's forehead.

The young man mumbled incoherently.

Beau looked back to Epione, whose hands still rested on the staff on Kaden's chest.

"We'll have to make sure he gets cleared by the doctors, but I don't think it should be a problem." Epione lifted her hands and moved them up Kaden's body. She lowered the hospital blanket and exposed the blue gown that covered him. She lifted the gown and exposed the young man's chest and the medley of wires and patches that laced over him.

She hummed contentedly as she pulled the lead wires from his chest.

"What are you doing?" Beau sounded upset.

"Don't worry. He's going to be okay."

Ariadne's heart beat fast in her chest as she looked up to Beau and saw the tears that welled in his eyes.

"Is he really going to be okay?" Beau looked down at Kaden.

Kaden's eyes flickered open. He looked up to Beau. "Dad?" he asked weakly.

"Yeah, buddy. I'm here. I'll always be here."

Chapter Twenty-Four

A week filled with hundreds of lab tests and many whispers about "miracles" had flown by. The nurses kept looking over at Kaden and murmuring together as they stood around the station at the center of the rehab unit.

Ariadne lifted Beau's hand and laced her fingers between his as they watched Kaden's mother, Lynda. She kept following Kaden as he pushed the IV stand around the hallway as if it were a weight holding him down.

"She's never going to forgive herself for not coming sooner." Beau pointed at Lynda. "She's a flake, but I guess she didn't realize how serious it was. I swear I tried to tell her. And now she's going to be trying to make it up to him forever."

"He's a great kid." Ariadne smiled. "He'll forgive her."

Beau looked down at their entwined fingers. "He knows what kind of person she is."

"I'm just glad he's going to stay here on the island with us." He soft lips pressed against the back of her hand. "I'll look for a job, maybe I can get hired at a university here?"

His lips trailed over her skin.

Ariadne pulled his hand to her face and rested her chin on their fingers. "Maybe I can pull some strings for you."

"I'll do it on my own. We're a team, but I can't depend on you for everything. You've already done so much for us." Beau smiled.

She smiled as she thought about her new life—a life with a purpose. No longer was she a mere nymph, a seductress. She would be at Epione's beck and call, when her goddess needed help in her healing.

Beau's phone rang from his pocket. With a look of shock, he answered. "Hello, Professor Ryan?"

There was a mumble from the other end of the line. Beau smiled. "Yes, about the tablet. I'm glad you deciphered it."

Another mumble.

"It talks about the Labyrinth?" Beau chuckled. "Well, I'm sorry to say…but the tablet was a hoax." He looked over at her and winked. "One of my students thought it would be funny."

The mumble grew louder.

"I understand. I'll be back to the university at the end of the summer to retrieve my things." Beau clicked the phone shut and stuffed it into his pocket. "I guess I will definitely need a new job."

She looked to Beau. "Thank you." Her heart filled with love. "But, about the curse—"

Beau stopped her as he pushed his lips against hers. She melted beneath his touch.

He pulled back as Epione swished into the room. Her white skirt billowed and flowed with a glorious swirl; she was the perfect goddess—beautiful, elegant, and kind.

Epione gazed around the rehab unit until she saw them sitting in the small waiting area. When she met Ariadne's eyes, she smiled knowingly, and then glided toward them. "I'm glad to see he's doing so well." She pointed at Kaden. "He's a fine young man."

"He is," Beau said with a proud nod. "But I don't know what I'm going to do about him and Trina. She doesn't want to come around anymore because of the curse. Seeing him hurt was especially hard on her. Kaden loves her."

"I know. She came to me last night, but I may have a solution that will work for her and you as well." Epione reached down into her white alligator skin purse and pulled out a small black velvet bag. "You must tell no one what I'm about to give you. There's not enough for every nymph." Epione lifted a small clear rock from the bag.

"You have proven yourself to be trustworthy, and without a doubt you will continue to do so. You have given up your dreams to fall in love with the unlovable. You are a fine man. And so I reward your valiance with this gift—a chip from the crystal staff." The goddess extended her hand and dropped the rock into Beau's palm. "This chip will keep you in good health for as long as it is in your possession. With this, I grant you a long life and good health. May you use it wisely."

Ariadne clamped her hand over her mouth. "My goddess…"

Epione smiled brightly as she took Ariadne's other hand. "Thank you for standing up for what is right. It is not always the easy thing to do, but you trusted your heart."

Ariadne didn't know what to say. After a moment, she forced her mouth to form a sound. "Thank you."

Epione brushed her lips against Ariadne's cheek. "You're welcome, my sister. I look forward to our future, bringing hope to those in need."

"Thank you." Beau stared at the crystal in his hand. "I can never repay all of you for what you've done."

Epione turned back to Beau. "Take care of my sister. Live peacefully at her side and follow wherever true love leads you. That is thanks enough." Epione kissed his cheek. "We shall meet again."

The goddess' eyes glistened and she turned away and made her way to the door. Kaden waved at her. Epione brought her fingers to her lips and blew him a kiss. "Blessed be, Kaden."

The door closed behind her. Ariadne looked to Beau and caught him brushing a tear from his cheek.

Kaden looked back at them as Lynda fussed, unaware, at his wayward faded black hair. Kaden reached into the front pocket of his hospital gown and lifted out a small crystal that was almost identical to the one Beau held in his hand.

The door opened. Trina raced in. "Kaden?"

She ran to him and threw her arms around him. "I love you, Kaden."

Lynda stepped back, a shocked look upon her face.

"Do you think she's going to be okay?" Ariadne pointed in Lynda's direction.

Beau laughed. "She's going to have to be."

Her heart clenched in her chest as she thought about how happy they all were. For once she had done something right. She took Beau's empty hand. "Thank you, Beau. Thank you for trusting me. And I hope you can forgive me for the mistakes I've made." A tear slipped down her cheek.

Beau reached over and wiped the wetness from her skin. "You've made some mistakes, but haven't we all? You're a wonderful person, and I'm glad to have you in my life." His thumb stroked over her lips. "Ariadne, I love you."

Beau pulled her hands to his lips. "Damn it, Ariadne. Say it. I know you feel the same way I do. I love you."

The hot tears fell unchecked. "I love you too, Beau."

He stood up and pulled her up and into his strong body. He took her lips with his. The kiss deepened. He pulled back, but kept his lips on hers. "I love you."

Kaden whistled. "Way to go, Dad!"

Beau snickered and she could feel the vibration of his laughter deep in her core. He pulled further back, but his arms held her tight. "Ariadne, I want to marry you."

She looked up at him. "What?"

"You heard me. Do you want to marry me?" Beau smiled and his eyes sparkled. In that moment, he was the most handsome man she had ever seen.

"Yes." It was the only thing she could say before she pulled him back down to her lips.

Ariadne let the moment take her. It didn't matter that the nurses, Lynda, Kaden, and Trina were watching, for a moment she let him have her. She was his—and he was her one true love.

About the Author

Danica Winters is a best-selling romance author who is known for writing award-winning books that grip readers with their ability to drive emotion through suspense and often a touch of magic. She is also the Marketing and Promotions Manager for Books to Go Now publishing. When she's not working, she can be found in the wilds of Montana testing her patience while she tries to understand the allure of various crafts (quilting, pottery, and painting are not her thing). She always believes the cup is neither half-full nor half-empty, but it better be filled with wine.

Please feel free to contact her through her website (*www.DanicaWinters.net*), Facebook (*www.Facebook.com/DanicaWinters*) or Twitter (*www.Twitter.com/DanicaWinters*).

In the mood for more Crimson Romance? Check out *Rhapsody* by Sharon Clare at *CrimsonRomance.com*.